A NOTE TO PARENTS

When your children are ready to "step into reading," giving them the right books is as crucial to their development as giving them the right food to eat. **Step into Reading®** books feature exciting stories and information reinforced with lively, colorful illustrations that make learning to read fun, satisfying, and rewarding. We have even taken the extra steps to keep your child engaged by offering Step into Reading Sticker books, Step into Reading Math, and Step into Reading Phonics books, in addition to fabulous fiction and nonfiction.

Learning to read, Step by Step:

- **Super Early** books (Preschool–Kindergarten) are perfect for emergent readers, with very large type and a word or two of super-simple text per page.
- **Early** books (Preschool–Kindergarten) let new readers tackle one or two short sentences of large type per page.
- **Step 1** books (Preschool–Grade 1) have the same easy-to-read type as Early, but with more words per page.
- **Step 2** books (Grades 1–3) offer longer and slightly more difficult text, introducing contractions and clauses. Children are often drawn to our exciting natural science nonfiction titles at this level.
- **Step 3** books (Grades 2–3) introduce paragraphs, chapters, and fully developed plot lines in fiction and nonfiction.
- **Step 4** books (Grades 2–4) feature thrilling nonfiction illustrated with exciting photographs for the increasingly independent reader.

Remember: The grade levels assigned to the six steps are intended only as guides. Some children move through all six steps rapidly; others climb the steps over a period of a few years. Either way, these books will help children "step into reading" for life!

Copyright © 2002 Disney Enterprises, Inc./Pixar Animation Studios. All rights reserved under International and Pan-American Copyright Conventions. Published in the United States by Random House, Inc., New York, and simultaneously in Canada by Random House of Canada Limited, Toronto, in conjunction with Disney Enterprises, Inc.

www.randomhouse.com/kids/disney

Library of Congress Cataloging-in-Publication Data:
Herman, Gail, 1959–
Boo on the loose / by Gail Herman.
    p. cm.— (Step into reading. Step 2 book)
SUMMARY: The number one Scare Team at Monsters, Inc., must come up with a solution when a girl named Boo makes her way onto the scare floor.
ISBN 0-7364-1274-3—ISBN 0-7364-8008-0 (lib. bdg.)
[1. Monsters—Fiction.] I. Title. II. Series.
PZ7.H4315 Bo 2002
[E]—dc21
2001031929

Printed in the United States of America   January 2002   10 9 8 7 6 5 4

STEP INTO READING, RANDOM HOUSE, and the Random House colophon are registered trademarks of Random House, Inc.

Step into Reading

DISNEY·PIXAR
MONSTERS, INC.
Boo on the Loose

A Step 2 Book

By Gail Herman

Illustrated by Scott Tilley,

Floyd Norman, and Brooks Campbell

Random House 🏠 New York

James P. Sullivan was
the top Scarer at Monsters, Inc.
Scaring kids was
an important job!
Kids' screams kept
the whole city running.

Sulley worked
on the Scare Floor.
He stood before a door
and waited for the signal.
The red light meant he could
open the door . . .

. . . and scare the kid

on the other side!

Big scares meant big screams.

Workers caught the screams.
Then the factory turned
the screams into energy.

Gas for cars.

Power for lights.

Sulley was heading home
at the end of his shift.
As he walked past
the Scare Floor,
he saw a door.

But all the doors

should have been put away.

"Is anybody there?" he said.

He peeked inside the room.

"Boo!" something said.

It was a little girl—

inside the monster world!

"Aaaah!" Sulley screamed.

Children were like
poison to monsters.
Every monster knew that.
Sulley tried to put the girl
back into her room.

But she kept popping out!

"Kitty!" she called to Sulley.

Sulley had to do something.

If anyone found out about her,

he could lose his job!

There was only one monster

Sulley could tell his secret to—

his best friend, Mike.

So Sulley took

the little girl home.

He sneaked her out in his bag.

Mike could not believe it!

A kid?

In their world?

"Her name is Boo," said Sulley.

"You <u>named</u> it?" cried Mike.

They had to get rid

of the dangerous kid.

So Mike came up with a plan.

The next morning,

they would drive her to the park

and try to lose her.

While she was sleeping,
Sulley and Mike peeked in on Boo.
"It is hard to believe she is
dangerous," said Sulley.
"Hey! That is <u>my</u> bear!" said Mike.

The next morning,

Sulley and Mike made

a monster costume for Boo.

Then they walked outside

to Mike's car.

"Be careful!" said Mike.

"Do not let that kid touch anything!"

When they got to the park,

Sulley and Mike got out of the car.

Mike went to open the door.

But Boo had locked herself in!

Mike was very angry!

"We have to get her out!"

he said.

Sulley had an idea.

He opened the trunk
and looked inside.

He found a spare tire.

"Time to play!" he said.

Sulley put Mike in the middle.

He rolled Mike all around.

"Fun!" Sulley said.

"Yeah, fun," Mike grumbled.

But Boo did not
get out of the car.

Next Sulley took out the car jack.
He cranked Mike up and down.
Boo still did not come out.
She was too busy playing
with Mike's bear.

Next Sulley swung Mike around.

"Don't <u>you</u> want to play, Boo?"

Sulley asked.

But nothing worked.

Boo waved

from inside the car.

"What do we do now?"

Mike shouted.

Just then,

a monster butterfly

flew past the car window.

Boo smiled and pointed.

Then she opened the car door

and ran after it!

The butterfly landed
on a fountain.
Boo tried to catch it.
But the butterfly was too fast.

Then the butterfly
flew into the woods.
Boo followed it.

Mike grabbed Sulley's arm.

"Now is our chance, Sulley!"

shouted Mike.

"Let's go!"

Mike tried to start the engine.

But the car would not start.

"We are out of gas!" said Mike.

But Sulley was not listening.

He was thinking about Boo.

He missed her already.

Then Sulley had an idea!

If Mike thought they needed Boo,

Sulley could get her back.

"We need to find Boo!"

Sulley said.

"Her scream will start the car."

Sulley ran into the woods.

"Boo?" Sulley called.

"I have your teddy bear. . . ."

Sulley did not see her anywhere.

"Boo, where are you?" he called.

Was she gone forever?

"Kitty?" said a small voice.

"Hi, Boo," said Sulley.

Boo ran right to him.

Boo hugged Sulley's leg.

Sulley smiled.

Boo did not seem

dangerous at all.

Sulley walked back to the car.

"You're holding its hand!"

Mike cried.

Sulley smiled.

"I know," he said.

"I feel okay, though."

Sulley helped Boo

into the car.

Then he got in, too.

"Now we need some scream,"

said Mike.

"Okay, Sulley," said Mike.

"You are the best Scarer

at Monsters, Inc.

Do your stuff!"

Sulley looked at Boo.

She smiled back at him.

He opened his mouth to roar . . .

but he could not do it.

He just could not scare little Boo!

"Just scare it, NOW!"

yelled Mike.

He banged his head

on the steering wheel.

HONK! went the horn.

"Ouch!" said Mike.

Boo laughed.

"Hee-hee-hee!"

The engine started with a roar!

Mike and Sulley looked at each other.

How did <u>that</u> happen?

Mike looked at Boo.

"Okay, she can stay for now,"

he said.

"But just remember,
that is <u>my</u> bear!"

CONTENTS

MATISSE
THE SENSUALITY OF COLOUR
Xavier Girard

THAMES AND HUDSON

'The story of my life is lacking in noteworthy events. Here it is in a nutshell. I was born on the last day of December 1869 in Le Cateau-Cambrésis (Nord). My parents, who were well-to-do shopkeepers, wanted me to enter the legal profession, so between the ages of eighteen and twenty-two I tried in good faith to be a law clerk in Saint-Quentin.'

Letter from Henri Matisse
to Frank Harris, 1921

CHAPTER 1

THE APPEAL OF PAINTING AND DRAWING

More felt than observed, *Landscape* (1895, opposite) shows that, for Matisse, outdoor scenes conveyed intimacy. The human figure would soon take the place of emotionally charged landscapes (academic study, 1892, right).

'But the town had a school for textile designers founded by [Maurice] Quentin de La Tour, and painting and drawing so strongly appealed to me that every morning, even in winter, I would get up to attend classes between 7 and 8 AM. Eventually my parents gave me leave to drop law and go to Paris to study painting.'

These words, from a 1921 letter, are as full an account of his life story as Matisse was ever to provide. When he chose to comment at length – which he did, in statements and writings, more often than many 20th-century painters – the topic would be art and the creative process, not his personal preferences or the byways of his personality.

'No thought of painting'

Henri-Emile-Benoît Matisse was born at 9 PM on 31 December 1869 in the house of his maternal grandparents at Le Cateau-Cambrésis in northern France. His parents, Emile-Hippolyte-Henri Matisse and Anna Heloïse Gérard, sold grain and paint in their store in the nearby hamlet of Bohain-en-Vermandois. It was there that Matisse spent his childhood.

If Matisse remembered much about his school days at the Collège de Saint-Quentin, he mostly kept it to himself. And if at school (1882–7) he showed any drawing aptitude, it was, as he told art historian Pierre Courthion in 1941, 'with no thought of painting at the time'. Both he and schoolmate Emile Jean (with whom he would later attend the Ecole des Beaux-Arts in Paris) were awarded first prize in drawing, an event he deemed memorable enough to mention years later, in 1952.

Matisse went to Paris to study law, passed his proficiency exam, and, 'little diploma' in hand, in 1889 went back home and began working as a clerk in the law office of

This snapshot in front of the Matisse-Gérard family store is one of the few photographs dating from Matisse's childhood. We can readily imagine the acrimonious discussions he must have occasioned in the Matisse-Gérard household when he announced he was going to be an artist. As a friend said much later, in 1952, 'He is still moved when he recalls the father he distressed and who never had any faith in him.' Although his parents and he did not always see eye to eye, Matisse did acknowledge that 'everything I have done comes from my parents, unassuming, hard-working folk'.

Maître Derieu, Place du Marché Couvert, in nearby
Saint-Quentin. But he was in poor health, and his time
there was interrupted by an acute attack of appendicitis.

essitaM .H

His operation required a fairly long convalescence, which
he spent in Bohain. It was there that he discovered
painting. The magic key had been turned. Matisse
was twenty-one, but his life had just begun.

A neighbour who ran a cloth-manufacturing firm
spent his leisure time copying landscapes reproduced in a
painting handbook. On his advice, Matisse took the paint
box his mother had given him and copied
pictures of a water mill and the entrance
to a village as painstakingly as he
would have transcribed a notarized
deed. In June 1890 he finished *Still
Life with Books* and signalled its
accuracy by

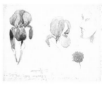

This watercolour of
irises on a notarized
document probably dates
from the late 1880s, when
Matisse was attending
classes at the Ecole
Quentin de La Tour.
Few subjects were to have
as telling an effect on
his own blossoming
career as that of flowers.
As he later told the critic
Ragnar Hoppe, 'Flowers
often leave impressions
of colour indelibly
burned on to my retina.'

Descended from
a family of
glovemakers and tanners,
Matisse's mother (with
her son in 1887, left)
tended the paint counter
in the family store. It
was probably through
her that Henri acquired
his taste for hats,
flowers (which she
painted on china) and
the decorative arts.

signing what he later called 'my first painting' with a mirror image of his own name ('essitaM .H').

Back at Maître Derieu's office, he took to decorating his papers with flowers and faces, just as he would years later in his illustrated books.

Every morning before work, Matisse attended a drawing class at the Ecole Quentin de La Tour, which specialized in tapestry and textile design. At lunchtime, he said, he would paint 'for an hour or so before returning to the office at two o'clock'. And then after work he would hurry back to his room 'and paint until nightfall'. He repeatedly visited Saint-Quentin's Musée Lecuyer, home to a famous collection of La Tour pastel portraits. In the museums of nearby Lille, Cambrai and Arras, he discovered the work of the Spanish painter Goya and the Dutch master Rembrandt, as well as northern European painting. He did many academic studies in the museums, but he also drew ornaments, which the Ecole Quentin de La Tour used as models for prospective curtain and fabric designers.

During this period he decorated the dining-room ceiling belonging to his Uncle Emile Gérard at Le Cateau. Later he would design a set of furniture for this room and would hang some copies he did in the Louvre on its walls.

Matisse was exempted from military service in

The law books featured in what Matisse called 'my first painting' (1890, above) represent the budding career that painting was destined to supplant.

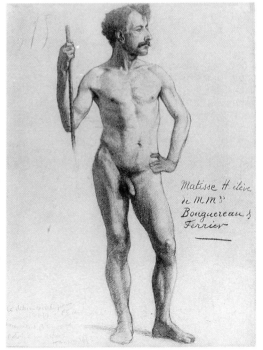

Matisse H élève de MM.rs Bouguereau & Ferrier

1889 because of continued poor health. At this time, he later said, 'I was completely alone, at liberty and at ease, whereas I had always been somewhat anxious and irked by all the things people would ask me to do.' In 1891 he reached a decision about his future. In the face of his father's disapproval, he abandoned the law, and with a letter of recommendation from a Saint-Quentin artist 'who painted hens and henhouses', he set off for Paris. There, in the autumn of 1891, Matisse met the influential conservative painter Adolphe-William Bouguereau.

'You'll starve!'

His father's words of warning still ringing in his ears – his allowance of a hundred francs a month was barely

Emile Jean and Jean Petit, flanking Matisse at the Académie Julian (below), were only the first of many friends who won the artist's unconditional devotion during his student years.

Opposite below: Matisse's approach to drawing in 1892 was wholly consistent with academic guidelines, as can be seen from this *Standing Nude*.

enough to keep hunger at bay – Matisse enrolled in the Académie Julian on 5 October 1891.

His introduction to Bouguereau took place while the professor, surrounded by his students, was at work on a copy of a copy of his painting *The Wasp's Nest*. 'During my first lesson,' Matisse later told Pierre Courthion, 'Bouguereau reprimanded me for using my finger to smudge a charcoal sketch and for placing my drawing badly on my sheet of paper.' Until such time as he could 'hold a pencil' correctly and 'master perspective', he was told he would never learn to draw. Matisse worked from a live model under Gabriel Ferrier, but this teacher's corrections proved equally unhelpful.

Yet Bouguereau and Ferrier sponsored Matisse in February 1892 as a candidate for the Ecole des Beaux-Arts entrance exam, which he failed. Probably at his teachers' urging, he registered that year for evening classes at the Ecole des Arts Décoratifs, where he attended 'a course in descriptive geometry for prospective drawing professors' and forged his long-lasting friendship with painter Albert Marquet. During this period, he often fretted over the prospect of not making good and of having to pick up where he had left off back home.

Matisse was torn by conflicting impulses. Although a student determined to master traditional techniques and open to the traditions of the Ecole, he was a free man, ready to make a break with the past.

An admirable master

Ironically, it was within the walls of the Ecole des Beaux-Arts – in the studio of Symbolist painter Gustave Moreau, which he unofficially joined late in 1892 – that he discovered the middle ground where his two sides could coexist.

While Matisse had been striving to draw in a manner consistent with academic standards – the descriptive, selective approach based on a detached awareness of the model – Moreau instead encouraged him to look inwards. He steered him toward the Mannerist tradition,

The French art critic and writer Louis Vauxcelles described Gustave Moreau's studio in the 1890s as 'a cohort so cultivated it verged on the Byzantine', a far cry from the rest of the Ecole des Beaux-Arts, 'a factory that turns out Prix de Rome [travelling fellowships]'. Above: Matisse and fellow Ecole students, c. 1893.

'Attendance at the Ecole should be replaced by leisurely outings at the zoo. There, through constant observation, students would learn about embryonic life, its secrets, its shudderings. They would gradually acquire those powers which real artists come to possess.'
          Letter from Henri
      Matisse to André Verdet
                      1952

as reformulated by Symbolism: to represent the concept of an object, irrespective of its actual visual appearance.

Before long, Matisse's challenge would be to find a way to reconcile the idealized Mannerist style, naturalistic rendering of the model, and his weakness for ornament. The fact that he always acknowledged his debt to

In this *Studio Interior* (c. 1898–9), the fixtures of academic training – model and studio – are rendered in bright colours, an intimation of lessons yet unlearned.

classical antiquity attests to this split. As he pointed out to his son Jean in 1926, 'I am sorry you don't want to draw from antique sculpture, for there you will find fully developed, three-dimensional form.'

Moreau's studio was a peaceful place. The painter Georges Rouault said it was remarkable for the 'gentle intellectual glow' that radiated from the man whom the painter Henri Evenepoël described as the 'charming master, with his white beard, smiling face, alert little eyes, and good-natured demeanour'. Unlike the Ecole's other professors, who could be so cold and cutting, Moreau taught with a passionate intensity as contagious as it was inexhaustible. Matisse later recalled that his teacher 'was capable of enthusiasm and even of getting carried away'. The man who Rouault said acted 'most like a master and least like a professor' discerned in each

Painted between 1897 and 1903, Matisse's copy (bottom) of Chardin's *The Ray* (1728, below) marked the decisive transition from careful practice copies to less literal variations on his own pictures.

'It's extremely complicated,' Matisse later told Pierre Courthion, referring to the Jan Davidsz. de Heem still life *La Desserte* (above), which he copied (left). 'It looks as if it were painted under a magnifying glass. Certain things in it are rendered in infinitesimal detail. So I set up my easel at the other end of the room and worked as if I were painting from life.' This copy was the basis for the huge *Variation on a Still Life by de Heem*, which Matisse painted in 1915 'according to the methods of modern construction'.

and every one of his students a seeker whose concepts of art were bound to stray from the way the Ecole, its teachers and inevitably even Moreau himself defined it.

Copying was an indispensable part of this phase of a young artist's apprenticeship. Marquet turned out studies after Poussin, Velázquez and Claude Lorraine; Evenepoël copied works by Rembrandt, Botticelli and Tintoretto.

Matisse decided instead to focus on still lifes by Chardin. In years to come, he based no fewer than five paintings on them.

Copying the old masters

His choice hardly comes as a surprise. Matisse had seen work by Chardin not only in the museum at Lille but also in 1892 in Paris at the Galerie Georges Petit. He was on familiar ground. The 'palpable gravity' of Chardin's paintings and their 'devotion to objects' (in the words of the novelist and critic André Gide) won him over immediately. Wasn't Chardin an extension of the northern European tradition, which held such appeal for Matisse? Hadn't Chardin achieved the very thing towards which Matisse himself would be working – those 'marriages of objects' aimed at fostering a state of pure contemplation unencumbered by theory?

Matisse proceeded, he said, to investigate 'gradations of tones in that silvery range favoured by the Dutch masters, the possibility of learning how to make light sing out within a subdued [colour] harmony and how most effectively to marshal [tonal] values'. A copy he did after the Dutch painter Jan Davidsz. de Heem's *La Desserte* combines the exuberance of a Flemish still life and the chromatic subtleties of 'Dutch rendering'.

He also painted literal copies aimed at generating cash (at a time when, as he later recalled, 'a decent copy fetched two to three hundred francs'). Matisse's repertoire ranged from the French Rococo to the Italian Renaissance to the Dutch masters.

In the end, Matisse copied out of his abiding affection for his freely chosen master and out of his own need for systematic analysis. His free interpretations afforded him the opportunity to experiment along more radical lines. His pen-and-ink study of Delacroix's *Abduction of Rebecca* reverses the scale of tonal values, replacing highlights with shadows, and vice versa.

The call of the open air

'I had two windows,' Matisse told Pierre Courthion, describing the cramped apartment at 19, Quai Saint-Michel, into which he moved shortly after his arrival in Paris. 'They overlooked the smaller arm of the Seine five storeys below. Lovely view: Notre-Dame to the right, the Louvre to the left, the Palais de Justice and the Préfecture

This portrait medallion of Caroline Joblaud from 1894 was Matisse's first attempt at sculpture.

Backdrop of many paintings between 1900 and 1914, the Quai Saint-Michel (below) amounted to an extension of Matisse's studio. He almost invariably left out the pedestrians and traffic and treated the historic landmarks as objects in a still life.

Painted at Beuzec-Cap-Sizun during Matisse's first trip to Brittany in 1895, *Village in Brittany/Peasant Woman Tending Pigs* proclaims the painter's debt to Corot, filtered through the work of Camille Pissarro and probably Jean-François Millet as well. An obstacle course sprang up between landscape and painter. The first step in his method is to spell out the problems – how best to paint against the light, against a broad expanse of sky? One solution is to place an enclosure of houses, roofs and steeples around the Breton peasant woman.

straight ahead.' The building was home to a regular 'caravansary of painters': Marquet, a neighbour off and on until the end of the war; Jacqueline Marval, invariably 'dressed as though it were Bastille Day'; a nephew of Corot's, a relative of Manet's. Matisse's studio, Moreau noted when he called on him there, revolved entirely around painting.

In 1893 Matisse began living with a young woman named Caroline Joblaud; she gave birth to their daughter the following year. Marguerite was to be an alert eyewitness to, and a principal player in, her father's oeuvre until the day he died.

On 1 April 1895 Matisse was finally admitted to the Ecole des Beaux-Arts, coming forty-second out of the eighty-six accepted candidates. Formal acceptance had no effect on his life-style or his relations with his family – only, now that the Ecole had officially opened its doors to him, he was seized by a sudden, irresistible craving for the open air. Whatever it was he sought to express could no longer be found in the Louvre. Hadn't Moreau told him that the process of self-discovery lay as much in the streets as in the studio? Didn't he keep talking about the need to throw out 'old rubbish'? Might not 'that beauty the masters did not render' be found in 'the mystery-shrouded ensemble formed by the Pont-Neuf and its trees, set against Notre-Dame?', as he wrote to Gustave Moreau. His early views of the Seine and the paintings by J. M. W. Turner he discovered soon afterwards in England were to prove that it could.

That summer, with his neighbour, the painter Emile Wéry as his guide, Matisse travelled west to the Brittany coast and set up his easel outdoors at Belle-Ile and Beuzec-Cap-Sizun. His rather diffident attempts at open-air painting during his first excursion smack of 'a timid Corot', to quote the art historian Pierre Schneider. No hint of Gauguin or his circle in Matisse's work, even though he visited the area where Gauguin painted. Instead, he favoured the placid seascapes so popular among Dutch painters, making no attempt to depict the seething, frothy waters of the Breton shore that others had so expertly rendered.

First of the portraits 'seen from the back', *Woman Reading* is reminiscent of Corot's studio scenes. The model, Caroline Joblaud, is surrounded by objects from the apartment-studio that she and Matisse shared.

The subdued atmosphere of *Woman Reading* (1895) and of the still lifes Matisse painted that year derived not from the Impressionists, but from Chardin. And the glowing lighting of his early studio interiors attests to the influence of the Corot retrospective he had seen before he left Paris. Matisse's sincere efforts at painting interiors and genre subjects helped in his election, at the age of twenty-six, as an associate member of the Société Nationale des Beaux-Arts on the recommendation of its president, Pierre Puvis de Chavannes.

Admiring only painting

Matisse's second trip to Belle-Ile, in the summer of 1896 (this time with Caroline, Marguerite and Emile Wéry), was markedly different from the previous year's hesitant attempts at open-air painting.

He had already begun to outgrow his role as the 'humble pupil' from the Moreau studio. Soon after his admission to the Ecole des Beaux-Arts, Matisse had exhibited work at the Salon de la Société Nationale des Beaux-Arts and received a commission from the French government. Events were proving him right at last.

Buoyed by newfound confidence, he visited Paris galleries where he saw Rembrandts, Goyas and other paintings on view. He met the painters of his day, among them the elderly father of Impressionism, Camille Pissarro: the same 'humble and colossal Pissarro' (to quote Paul Cézanne) who had introduced Gauguin to open-air painting and whom Cézanne and Vincent van Gogh had consulted. Indeed, Pissarro, who exerted his quiet authority over the Neo-Impressionists (known for covering their canvases with areas of pure colour) was an ideal guide for Matisse. The point of equilibrium between Chardin, the Impressionists and Cézanne (whose importance he was probably the first to impress upon Matisse), Pissarro was the consummate exponent of that cultivated, seasoned, deliberate Impressionism towards which Matisse was heading at the time.

'I worked at Belle-Ile,' Matisse later told novelist and critic Raymond Escholier, 'on the wild coastline Monet painted,' shown here in the expansive *Seascape at Goulphar* (1896). 'At the time all I had on my palette was bistre and earth colours, whereas Wéry had an Impressionist palette.... I found the brilliance of pure colour captivating.'

Opposite below: an 1896 photograph of Matisse at Belle-Ile.

'I was looking for myself,' Matisse later said of his formative years. He investigated several artistic options, from cautiously attempting to emulate the Impressionists Monet and Pissarro to using incendiary colours inspired by Van Gogh and Redon. He used space in the style of Cézanne, experimented with colours according to Signac's advice and followed the example of Puvis de Chavannes. Finally, his own intuition showed him the way.

CHAPTER 2

THE ALLURE OF THE EXOTIC

The title of the painting *Luxe, Calme et Volupté* (1904–5, detail opposite) – taken from Baudelaire's poem 'L'Invitation au voyage' – alludes to a state of bliss arising from the spontaneous harmony between the landscape and the female nudes. Right: Matisse's first self-portrait (1900–3) was inspired by Rembrandt.

When, in late 1896, Gustave Moreau advised his student to undertake a 'masterpiece' that would cap five years of training, Matisse naturally decided on an interior scene. The bravura *Dinner Table*, first in a series of paintings of laid sideboards, was one of five paintings he exhibited at the Salon de la Société Nationale in 1897.

'My friend Matisse is doing Impressionist work and has Claude Monet on the brain,' Evenepoël wrote to a friend on 2 February 1897. 'Hucklenbroich, one of Moreau's more understanding students, defends him.' So did Moreau, but it was no use. Matisse took such early taunts to heart, wondering if he was heading down the wrong path.

Shrugging off the yoke of academicism

When Impressionist and Post-Impressionist paintings from the bequest of Gustave Caillebotte were put on view in Paris, Pissarro and Matisse went to see them. This contact with Impressionist paintings, combined with a third trip Brittany, bolstered the young artist's confidence in the choices he had made.

Then, in Matisse's work, the consistency of colour and texture so favoured by Pissarro began to shatter, as if in reaction to his exposure to Neo-Impressionist fragmentation. '[Pure] rainbow colours' suddenly appeared in *The Port of Le Palais, Belle-Ile* (1896) in a still-evolving palette of violet, red, turquoise and cadmium yellow.

In late 1897 Matisse ended his liaison with Caroline Joblaud but legally recognized Marguerite as his daughter. He had already met Amélie Parayre, a young woman from Toulouse, whom he

'While I was in Gustave Moreau's studio, I thought I would never do figures,' Matisse told Louis Aragon. 'So I put figures in my still lifes.' Although the Pissarro-inspired Impressionist technique of *The Dinner Table* (1896–7, left) is remarkable in its own right, the painting's real significance lies in the combination of two types of painting that Matisse had until then investigated independently. Below centre: *The Port of Le Palais, Belle-Ile* (1896). Opposite and below: Henri Matisse and Amélie Parayre in 1898.

later described as 'erect, dignified of bearing, and possessed of splendid dark hair'. He proposed to her that autumn, and on 8 January 1898, they were married in Paris.

Matisse's trips to Brittany and the completion of *The Dinner Table* had widened the gap between him and the Ecole. The aged Moreau himself faded into the background, albeit under protest. 'Good old Moreau is much changed and showing his age,' wrote fellow student Jules Flandrin on 19 November 1897. 'Not that he refrains from reprimanding (to put it mildly) self-indulgent students who have been overly bold with the brush. It all started with Matisse, who brought in an enormous amount of hard work after the holidays, steeped in the countryside and the open air.'

Matisse's reaction was not long in coming. He decided to give himself 'a year's respite', as he later wrote, 'during which time I resolved to brush aside all impediments and paint as I saw fit. I worked for nobody but myself. I was saved.'

His marriage provided Matisse with an excuse to get out of Paris. Heeding Pissarro's advice, the young couple spent their honeymoon in London, where Matisse was able to see paintings by Turner. Then, in February 1898, shortly after they returned to Paris, they were off again, this time for Ajaccio, Corsica.

Corsican Landscape (1898), painted during Matisse's stay in Ajaccio (c. 1900, below).

The wondrous south

The days of the 'flitting dilettante' were behind him. No longer was it enough to 'drift from Rembrandt to Corot, from Veronese to de Heem and Chardin', as he said in 1949. The 'old ways of painting' could not do justice to the immediacy of his feelings.

'So,' he said, 'off I went into the back of beyond to forge my own, simpler means that wouldn't stifle me spiritually.' Matisse left the Ecole, the Salons and the museums behind and began to rely on himself. His journey to Corsica was part of the quest for intuitive self-revelation that absorbed many *fin-de-siècle* artists.

In Corsica, he re-energized himself beneath the overwhelming Mediterranean sun. 'I was amazed,' he later proclaimed. 'Everything shone, all was colour, all was light.' Here, as in Brittany, he divided his time between interior scenes and landscapes.

The trips to Brittany had been Matisse's initiation into open-air landscape painting, his 'revelation of light in nature'. In Corsica, where the countryside fairly effervesced with colour, he felt the need to reintroduce the palpable qualities of light. At once exuberant and focused, *The Courtyard of the Mill* (1898, above) attempts to show the effect of sunshine on an enclosed area awash with 'rainbow colours'.

But self-abandonment came with its share of self-restraint and last-minute second thoughts. Far from allowing the intense colour and light of the outdoors to surge unchecked, Matisse sought to contain the overflow within the confines of *pochades*, quick colour paintings that intentionally narrow the field of view by means of a wall or clump of foliage. The examples of his work that he dispatched to Evenepoël left his friend dumbfounded. How could Matisse, so 'skilful in the art of greys', that past master of 'singular, powerful harmonies', have turned out such 'exasperated painting' worthy of a 'deranged, epileptic Impressionist'?

On 18 April 1898, while Matisse was still in Corsica, his aged teacher, Moreau, died. But Matisse waited until June to return to Paris. He spent just that month in the capital, but managed to take in the Salon des Indépendants (where Paul Signac dominated the Neo-Impressionist contingent), the Monet exhibition at the Galerie Georges Petit, and the Cézannes on view at Ambroise Vollard's gallery.

Soon after their return to Ajaccio in July, Matisse and his wife, now pregnant with their son Jean, went to Beauzelle, near Toulouse, to stay with her family for six months. Monet's canvases and Van Gogh's landscapes were still fresh in his mind when he painted the banks

The lengthened format of *Street in Toulouse* (1899, above), which Matisse painted after his return from Corsica, attests to the impact of Japanese prints on his work around the turn of the century. 'We kept away from the Louvre,' he wrote to his friend André Rouveyre, 'for fear of being put on the wrong track, or, rather, of getting sidetracked. But we did look at the Japanese because of the colour they had to show'. Although Matisse's exposure to Japanese prints was limited to 'cheap reprints' he purchased, their aesthetic taught him that 'colour exists in itself [and] has a beauty of its own'.

of the Garonne River. The still lifes from that summer suggest that he had read Signac's landmark writing on Neo-Impressionism, then appearing serially in the prominent journal *La Revue blanche*. These articles enabled him to assess not only the progress he had already made, but the place he might eventually make for himself in a genealogy of colourists that included Manet, Renoir, Monet, Pissarro, Seurat and Cézanne.

Many of Matisse's friends were painters. Top: Charles Camoin and Albert Marquet. Above: Henri Manguin.

First Orange Still Life (1899, left) was probably influenced by Van Gogh and Gauguin, but also by Signac. Impressionism's 'subtle gradations of tone' are here overwhelmed by the tonality that inspired the poet Guillaume Apollinaire to describe the orange as 'a fruit bursting with light'. The objects are clustered toward the centre, as if trying to hold out against the onslaught of orange.

'Learning about volume by touch alone'

Once back in Paris in early 1899, however, he made a beeline for the Ecole des Beaux-Arts. A string of professors – no fewer than six in one year – had been unable to fill Moreau's shoes. Eventually, Fernand Cormon took over, but Moreau's former students scattered.

Matisse cast about for 'study options'. His first stop was the Académie Julian, 'but I was forced to beat a hasty retreat', he noted, 'because the students held my studies up to ridicule'. Off he went to a studio a model named Camillo had opened and where Eugène Carrière came to work with his private students.

'The [Académie Camillo],' Matisse recalled, 'was where I met Jean Puy, [Pierre] Laprade, [Jean] Biette, [André] Derain, [Auguste] Chabaud; not a single student of Moreau's was there.' When the studio where 'one could finally work in complete peace and quiet' closed, he found a haven at Biette's place on the Rue Dutot. There were also life-drawing classes at the Académie Colarossi, where for fifty centimes he would dash off what Pierre Schneider has described as 'instant academy figures' to the sound of piano music.

He worked there for two whole years, drawing anatomical studies and, as he later told the poet and writer Louis Aragon, working with his eyes closed, 'learning about volume by touch alone'. Before long, he was rounding out these sessions with evening sculpture classes at the Académie de la Grande-Chaumière under Antoine Bourdelle. In addition, he and Marquet worked outdoors in the Luxembourg Gardens, on the banks of the Seine and in the streets. In the afternoons he could be found drawing cabaret singers auditioning.

One day, a friend from the Moreau studio, Marie-Vital Lagare, took Matisse to meet the famous sculptor Auguste Rodin – a disappointing

One of Matisse's oldest friends, Albert Marquet (on the left in the photograph opposite, playing chess with Eugène Druet), has been described as 'retiring and taciturn' with a 'marked taste for brevity in word, thought, and deed'.

At Moreau's prodding, Matisse and Marquet went into the streets together, sketching horses at rest (below) and other scenes of everyday life. Matisse destroyed many of these drawings in 1936.

H Matisse

experience. Rodin was not Pissarro. But no matter, thought Matisse. The person who created *The Walking Man* was a 'very great sculptor' just the same.

During this period Matisse painted *Still Life Against the Light* (1899), an early example of his 'symphonic' approach to painting. He would try out incompatible options simultaneously, putting one on hold, returning to another later on, discarding still another along the way, only to reactivate and synthesize them elsewhere later on.

The bridge Matisse could see from his window is featured in a series of cityscapes (1900–5). The milky opalescence Marquet favoured in similar scenes has given way to a shorthand of bright, schematic colour planes flung across a luminously backlit canvas, part of which has been left unpainted in *Pont Saint-Michel* (c. 1900, below).

Cézanne: 'the father of us all' (Picasso)

The year of 1899 also found Matisse visiting avant-garde galleries – and Ambroise Vollard's in particular – where

Probably no work of art sustained Matisse more often than Cézanne's *Three Bathers* (1879–82, left). The artist bought the canvas in 1899 and refused to part with it for thirty-seven years, until it was donated to the Musée du Petit Palais. A seamless melding of figure and landscape, Cézanne's painting harmonizes human forms with their natural setting, a tightly controlled pictorial totality subordinating visible reality.

he bought Cézanne's *Three Bathers*, Rodin's plaster bust of Henri Rochefort and Gauguin's *Head of a Boy* in rapid succession. Becoming the owner of *Three Bathers* marked the end of his unfocused fascination with Cézanne and the beginning of a personal relationship with the oeuvre of the master of Aix. His influence

Matisse was nearly carried away by what the art critic Félix Fénéon heralded as 'the frenzied triumph of the sun', only to settle down to the task of disciplining it. Drawing on the lessons of Marquet and the Symbolist painters, Matisse used backlighting in *Still Life Against the Light* (1899, left) to counteract the sensation of depth. Yet the same period witnessed *The Serf* (1900–4, opposite above, before the arms were removed, and below, after), all dents and bulges, a foil to the canvases that flattened and equalized space through colour.

would continue to be felt until the end of Matisse's career. He bought the Cézanne painting, he said, because of 'the proportion of the hand of the walking woman with respect to the composition as a whole'. He was suddenly called away from Paris 'because my child [Marguerite] was ill. While waiting to go back to Paris, I would go and watch soldiers bathing in the river. On the banks of the Garonne I recaptured that hand and its colour in the landscape'.

Cézanne versus Rodin: Matisse said that the sculptor worked by 'assembling fragments' that were in themselves 'admirable', but which showed little concern for the 'confusion of expression' they created. Every component of Cézanne's painting, however, was unambiguously orchestrated in accordance with a 'general architectural scheme' that gave the bather's hand and the landscape the same pictorial quality. Matisse's turn-of-the-century academic studies, as well as drawings or sculptures like *The Serf* and *Madeleine (I)* and *(II)*, suggest that he was torn between the expressive vehemence of Rodin and the discipline of Cézanne.

As if to keep this tug-of-war from getting out of hand,

between 1899 and 1903 Matisse studied the work of Rembrandt (then enjoying newfound popularity). Matisse created a number of pictures of himself during this period. They are not so much conventional self-portraits as likenesses of an artist who happens to be engraving, painting or sculpting as he gazes quizzically at himself. He also examined Marquet's painting, with its high viewpoints, spatial compression and delicate opalescent light.

Featured early in his career as framed pictures in *Woman Reading* and *Still Life with a Top Hat,* Matisse's self-portraits follow in the tradition of the old masters. This one (below) from 1900 is a portrait of the young painter as an impartial observer of himself.

In the north

Since Matisse's return from Toulouse, things had taken a distinct turn for the worse. The Salon de la Société Nationale rejected his submission. His copies of old masters stopped selling. Matisse, with Marquet, took a job painting decorations for the Grand Palais in preparation for the 1900 World's Fair. His father threatened to cut off his allowance.

The art dealer Paul Durand-Ruel suggested he paint 'interiors with figures' instead of still lifes too heavily influenced by Cézanne. 'The path of painting seemed completely blocked to the younger generations,' Matisse later wrote to Raymond Escholier. 'The Impressionists were grabbing all the attention. No notice was taken of Van Gogh and Gauguin. A wall had to be knocked down to get through.'

On 13 June 1900 his second son, Pierre, was born. In the winter Matisse came down with bronchitis and went to Villars-sur-Ollon in Switzerland to recover. He brought back two little paintings he described as 'simple images'. When he got back he tried, and failed, to find work. Until 1903 he shuttled between Bohain-en-Vermandois, where his parents were caring for Jean, and Paris, where he occasionally attended drawing sessions. As a diversionary tactic, he reluctantly turned out anecdotal paintings in subdued colours, but sales – to the gallery owner Berthe Weill, the critic Félix Fénéon, Vollard (who bought *The Dinner Table*) and dealers Josse and

Ambroise Vollard (above) organized Matisse's first major one-artist exhibition in June 1904 and bought many of his early works at a time when the painter was without a contract.

A picture by Matisse is an evolving work space. Insistently repainted canvases like *Interior with a Harmonium* (1900, left) attest in an almost cinematic way to an ongoing, open-ended process of reconstruction. For example, in earlier versions the lower left corner of the harmonium had been tilted forward, splayed out and bisected by the lid, the edge of which completes a downward-pointing arrow. The book in the foreground would tip this gravity pointer slightly more towards the ground, were it not balanced by a bunch of roses thrust towards the interior of the room.

Gaston Bernheim – were lacklustre. 'If I had the chance,' he wrote on 10 August 1903, 'I think I'd give up painting.'

He applied for a position as 'entertainment tax assessor'. Even that fell through. In poor health, his wife was forced to close her 'none too flourishing' millinery shop, which she had opened to help make ends meet. In the summer, there seemed to be no alternative but to move back to Bohain. Matisse was not to return to Paris until the beginning of 1904.

Going south

'I am leaving tomorrow for Saint-Tropez with my wife and kid,' he wrote on 12 July 1904. Since his trip to

Toulouse, the prospect of 'stealing away to the south of France for a bit of relaxation' had been in the back of his mind. 'That is my fondest hope,' he confessed to a friend in 1903. 'I believe I'll get twice as much work done there as up north, where the light is so poor in winter.'

The south beckoned as a potential antidote to the difficult years between 1899 and 1903. But he found that

A bove: Paul Signac (c. 1907).

M atisse drew this Saint-Tropez landscape during the summer of 1904. Its noteworthy features are a view from above, a very high horizon line, a Japanese-style cut-off branch and the artist himself, who intrudes into the foreground. 'Very often I put myself in a picture and I am conscious of what exists behind me,' he later said. 'I express the space and objects which are situated there as naturally as if I were looking at only the sea and sky, that is, the simplest things imaginable.'

the 'glaring flood' of Mediterranean light about which his host, Paul Signac, had raved, not to mention the 'extremely hot weather', soon overwhelmed him. The only painting of any consequence Matisse managed to finish was a view of Signac's terrace, his first attempt at combining the more decorative aspects of Neo-Impressionism and Cézanne's architectonic use of colour. Here, Marquet's influence proved more telling than Signac's. Signac bluntly took Matisse to task for adopting an approach so far removed from Neo-Impressionism.

But Matisse came around to the Neo-Impressionist leader's way of thinking in *The Gulf of Saint-Tropez* (1904), which he painted at the Plage des Graniers, a beach not far from Signac's villa, La Hune.

Once Matisse was back in Paris, after the summer, *The Gulf of Saint-Tropez* would become the starting point for his next major statement, a painting whose decorative aspirations proclaim his debt to Puvis de Chavannes as well as to such Elysian Neo-Impressionist allegories as Signac's *Time of Harmony* and Henri-Edmond Cross' *L'Air du Soir*. By adopting their Arcadian imagery and precepts regarding colour, Matisse bowed with seeming humility before an aesthetic that had already been coordinated, codified and given official recognition.

Matisse's conflict with Paul Signac over *The Terrace, Saint-Tropez* (1904, above left) prompted him to paint *The Gulf of Saint-Tropez* (above right) in the same year. The difference between the two paintings suggests calculated backsliding. Despite, or because of, this reversion to Neo-Impressionism, *The Gulf of Saint-Tropez* turned Matisse's attention towards the 'enchanted shores' that his earlier Mediterranean landscapes at Saint-Tropez had ignored.

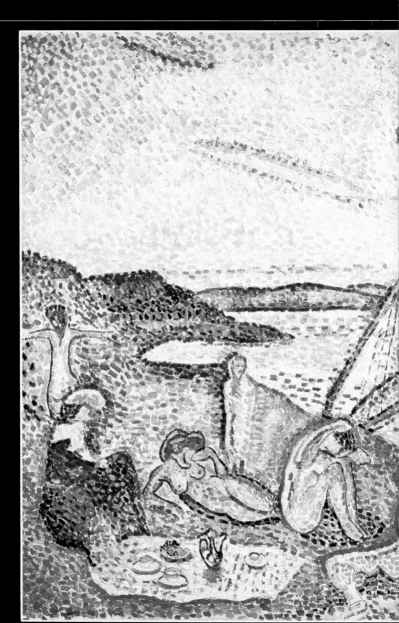

A bove: *Study of a Pine Tree* (1904).

L uxe, Calme et Volupté (1904–5) brings together three seminal themes in Matisse's oeuvre – classical antiquity, family and landscape – in a composition that unfolds like a slow-motion tracking shot. 'It is a canvas painted with pure rainbow colours,' Matisse later wrote. 'All the paintings of that school (Neo-Impressionism) produced the same effect: a little pink, a little blue, a little green; a very limited palette with which I did not feel very comfortable.'

Above: the cover of the twentieth Salon des Indépendants exhibition catalogue, 1904.

'Collioure? It has women, boats, the sea, and mountains,' Derain wrote in 1905. 'But most of all it has light. Golden blond light that obliterates shadows.' In *Interior at Collioure/ The Siesta* (1905, left), Matisse caught the light of the fishing village in a room overlooking the sea. His aim was to convey not the colour of objects in daylight, but a gentle swirling motion such as might be seen in a dream or a colourist's laboratory, a motion that unsteadies the walls and floor, disperses shadows and reflections and suffuses indoors and outdoors in an all-enveloping ring of hues. The landscape has stolen not only into the room, but also into the dream of the napping woman and the reverie of her counterpart on the balcony.

He had done this with his first masterpiece, *The Dinner Table*, back in the years 1896–7, and he did it again over the period 1904–5 with his next major painting, *Luxe, Calme et Volupté*. Matisse found that the distance the austere technique of Neo-Impressionism created between the painter and his subject opened up fresh possibilities for his imagination in the representation of nature.

The Fauve period

Exhibited at the Salon des Indépendants from March to April 1905, *Luxe, Calme et Volupté* received mixed reviews. Signac, who bought it that September, waxed rhapsodic. Hadn't he brought Matisse into the Neo-Impressionist fold? Jean Puy concurred, writing that Matisse, 'carried away' by a Signac exhibition in December 1904, had turned into a 'thoroughgoing Pointillist'.

But Louis Vauxcelles and the painter and writer Maurice Denis warned him against 'investigations that go against his true nature' and the 'pitfalls of abstraction'.

As the investigation by the writer Charles Morice into the future of art had demonstrated that year – he had asked artists of every aesthetic kind (though

not Matisse) for their opinions – Impressionism was running out of fresh ideas. A surfeit of contending techniques, styles, and methods filled the vacuum, eventually spawning *fin-de-siècle* decadence. Newfound innocence and primitivism seemed the only way out.

Matisse's answer was to head back south, to a remote part of France, nowhere near Signac: Collioure, a small seaport on the Mediterranean near the Spanish border.

'If [it] manages to combine the world outside, the sea and the world inside,**'** Matisse said of *The Open Window* (1905), 'it is because the atmosphere of the landscape and of my room are one and the same.'

On 15 May 1905 he checked himself, his wife and two of his children into a 'fairly cheap boarding house'. There, in a room overlooking the water, he set about painting the 'thrilling scenery' that Signac, who had visited the fishing village in 1887, had glowingly described.

When he arrived, the Seurat and Van Gogh retrospectives Matisse had recently seen in Paris were still fresh in his mind. He painted a pointillistic study of a young woman for use in a larger composition (*Woman with a Parasol*) and *Mme Matisse in the Olive Grove*, an attempt to graft Seurat's method on to Van Gogh's maelstrom of colour.

This scenario changed radically when in midsummer Matisse was joined by André Derain, a painter who had mastered the rules of the new, wildly colourful game of Fauvism. Derain described them in a letter:

'1) A new concept of light consisting in this: negation of shadows. Light here is very strong, shadows very

Matisse painted *Landscape at Collioure* (above) during the summer of 1905. 'Fauvism was a brief period during which we thought it necessary to exalt all colours together and sacrifice none of them.' *Collioure Landscape* (1905, opposite above) attempts to slow down the movement of the observer's eye into the distance by studding the bay with a succession of space-shearing sails. Opposite below: portrait of Matisse by André Derain (1905).

bright. Shadows are a whole world of brightness and luminosity that contrasts with sunlight: what we call reflections. Until now both of us have overlooked this, and as far as composition goes, it will enhance expression in the future.

'2) Noted, when working with Matisse, that I must root out obsession with divisionism. He keeps on using it, but I've got over it completely and hardly ever use it anymore. It makes sense in a luminous, harmonious picture but works against those things which owe their expression to intentional disharmony.'

A 'painfully dazzling' work of art

When Matisse returned to Paris early that autumn, he painted *The Woman with the Hat*, a picture of his wife that violently transposed into portraiture the high-keyed colours he had

unleashed in the Collioure landscapes. This painting, intended for the Salon d'Automne, was an academic portrait wrenched off course. It was the first of a long series, and everything about it spelled confrontation – with the public, who stared at it as if it were some Byzantine idol; with conservative Salon painters, whom it challenged; with Renoir and Manet, who were due for retrospectives; with his own paintings, the bulk of them small landscapes and still lifes; and with his wife, who dressed in black to sit for the portrait but was transformed into a radiant icon forced to contend with a riot of colour.

Maurice Denis described this – and all of Matisse's Salon paintings that year – as 'painfully dazzling'. Leo Stein, who later purchased it, initially thought it 'a thing brilliant and powerful, but the nastiest smear of paint I had ever seen'. Matisse himself had misgivings about the effect the portrait might have on his own work. His flaunting of colour had filled him with a kind of dread. Fauvism had led him beyond ordinary representation, into unexplored territory where the human face was

Through the juxtaposition of a hat (more landscape than headgear), a face and a Japanese fan, in *The Woman with the Hat* (1905, above left), like its retort, *Portrait of Mme Matisse/The Green Line* (1905, above right), Matisse sought not only to vie with the great portraits of Manet and Renoir, but to paint a human face as though it were a wild, jarring patchwork of distinct, yet equally intense compartments of colour.

violently infused with intense Mediterranean light. 'The truth is that painting is a very disappointing thing,' he noted at the time. 'My canvas (the portrait of my wife) happens to be enjoying limited success among the advanced. But it hardly satisfies me at all. It marks the beginning of a gruelling effort.'

The question of the Salon

Shortly after the Salon d'Automne opened, while the Fauvist controversy was in full swing, Matisse began work on *Le Bonheur de Vivre* (1905–6), another imaginary composition so big (174 x 238.1 cm) he had to rent a special work space to complete it. (He maintained this studio in the Couvent des Oiseaux at 56, Rue de Sèvres, until 1908.) Like *Luxe, Calme et Volupté*, *Le Bonheur de Vivre* articulated the broadest range of allusions and styles Matisse had attempted to that point in his career. The painting quickly became, to quote Charles Morice, 'the question mark of the Salon'. Louis Vauxcelles faulted its linearity and schematization. Signac denounced it vehemently. All the same, the canvas that was destined to be relegated to a stairwell in the Barnes Foundation had fulfilled Matisse's aim: to create a pictorial poem like the Symbolist poet Stéphane Mallarmé might have composed, one that was at once sensual and supremely abstract.

A complex of pictures within a picture as well as an eclectic mix of themes and iconographic sources ranging from prehistoric cave painting and classical mythology to Stéphane Mallarmé and a Parisian cabaret, *Le Bonheur de Vivre* (left) was Matisse's most important pictorial statement after *Luxe, Calme et Volupté*. Five months in the making, it consists of images that were independently conceived and subsequently arranged to create visual associations within a stage set of plant motifs. This transposition of Matisse's landscape of Collioure (p. 44) into a decorative key presents the Garden of Eden in planar, linear terms reminiscent of Symbolist stage flats that the painter Edouard Vuillard designed. Full of subtle rhymes and associations, the composition unfolds like a poem by Mallarmé. Despite the ring of dancers designed to pull its scattered fragments together, the picture's ambiguity and ultimate irresolution, combined with its Symbolist overtones, reflect a stage in Matisse's career at once transitional and bursting with potential.

Matisse returned to Collioure in May 1906 declaring – as if to justify Fauvism's reputation for wildness – that he was 'of a mind to paint everything to shreds'. He took up sculpture and ceramics and transposed that work on to canvas, and his paintings were soon veering towards the purely decorative. 'I kept trying to do two things at once,' he said a few years later.

CHAPTER 3

COLOUR, DANCE AND MUSIC

In *Harmony in Red/La Desserte* (1908, detail opposite), Matisse brought the consistency of realistically observed objects in tune with decorative abstraction and used carefully coordinated colour to reconcile disembodied linearity with weight and volume. *Reclining Nude* (1906, right), spread out over four sheets of paper, was probably the point of departure for his sculpture *Reclining Nude (I)*.

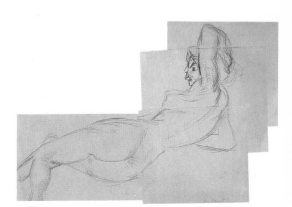

The Edenic reverie of *Le Bonheur de Vivre* lingered in small outdoor studies, loosely brushed Fauvist pastoral landscapes filtered through a Cézannesque lens. In the spring of 1906 Matisse travelled to Algeria, visiting Algiers, Constantine, Batna and Biskra, and was overwhelmed by all its beauty and light,

He returned to Collioure and spent the rest of the summer painting two versions of *The Young Sailor*. He began to feature images of sculpture in his canvases, which Cézanne had done as well.

Portrait of the painter as a sculptor

Using figures from *Le Bonheur de Vivre* as his point of departure, Matisse devoted most of the winter of 1906–7 to investigating the 'special demands sculpture makes with regard to volume and mass'.

The painter became engrossed in creating a sculpture, *Reclining Nude (I)*. But the clay model fell to the ground while it was being modelled. 'Stunned by the mishap,' Matisse decided to transpose the figure on to a large canvas and surround it with an imaginary Algerian oasis in remembrance of Biskra. (He returned to the sculpture later.)

The urgency of the transfer transported him. The explosive, primordial *Blue Nude: Memory of Biskra* (1907) is not merely a picture of a statuette, but a larger-than-life apparition that

A series of exchanges and transpositions led Matisse from *Reclining Nude (I)* (1906–7, below) to *Blue Nude: Memory of Biskra* (1907, opposite).

seems to have burst into the pictorial field by brute force.

As he had done in *The Woman with the Hat*, Matisse took a conventional pose – the one exemplified by Ingres' *Odalisque with Slave* (1839–40), Alexandre Cabanel's *The Birth of Venus* (c. 1863), and Manet's *Olympia* (1863) – and infused it with dramatic tension. Emphatic frontality, the conspicuously upthrust arm, and the equally insistent horizontality of the woman's bent legs create an impression of extreme anatomical distortion. The numerous areas that were repainted suggest that the figure was not so much painted as modelled on the two-dimensional surface. Despite Matisse's reliance on blue to create a sense of depth (a lesson learned from Cézanne), the canvas reads like a flattened surface

Fauvist Ariadne, colossal African odalisque and masculine nymph rolled into one, *Blue Nude: Memory of Biskra* (above) marshals inconsistent elements and interweaves them in a way that greatly intensifies the figure's formal and symbolic impact. The fact that the figure reemerged in the work of Picasso, Derain and Braque at this time attests to this painting's status as one of the seminal images of early Cubism.

Opposite left: Alexandre Cabanel's *The Birth of Venus*.

ornamented with violets, palm fronds and fig leaves, making *Blue Nude* an ultimately decorative work of art. The title it bore when Matisse submitted it to the 1907 Salon des Indépendants – *Tableau III (Painting III)*, his only entry that year – suggests that it was intended to be a follow-up to *Luxe, Calme et Volupté* and *Le Bonheur de Vivre*.

Surrounded by a border of vine leaves and bunches of grapes, a nymph (1907, left), the left part of the ceramic triptych for the Osthaus house, is the decorative sister of *Blue Nude: Memory of Biskra*. This little-known painted-and-glazed-tile mural was relegated to a small room, but its lessons were to stand the artist in good stead in his later work.

Crucible of creativity: ceramics

Having been brought up in a textile school, and having watched his mother painting plates, Matisse had become interested in pottery at an early age. He brought some pieces back from Algeria to France, and they turned up in his paintings soon afterwards. Therefore, the ceramics he coproduced with André Méthey in 1907 cannot be dismissed as a mere diversion. In any case, he was not the first painter to investigate this medium. Méthey had teamed up with Renoir, Redon, Pierre Bonnard and Maurice Denis earlier, and Gauguin had formed such a partnership with ceramicist Ernest Chaplet in 1886.

Around 1907 Matisse was commissioned to design a ceramic triptych for the house of Karl-Ernst Osthaus in Hagen, Germany. This decorative project, with its nymph and satyr, dancing female figures, and border of vine leaves and bunches of grapes, was to leave its imprint on not only the large-scale paintings of the next several years, but also on artwork Matisse produced late in life.

Painted ceramics lie at the core of Matisse's aesthetics in terms of both subject matter and simplification of technique. He featured them in such paintings as *Still*

Life with Asphodels (1907) and *The Girl with Green Eyes* (1908) and later made ceramic-tile murals an integral part of his architectural projects. 'I have colours and a canvas,' he later remarked, 'and I must express myself with purity even if it means doing so summarily, for example, with four or five spots of colour [and] four or five drawn lines possessed of plastic expression.' Line, pure colour, and the white ground of ceramic surfaces were combined as an exercise in creativity, as a way to fully tap the expressive potential of intense blues, oranges and reds.

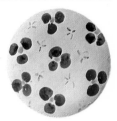

Matisse teamed up with ceramicist André Méthey in 1907 to produce a series of plates, dishes and vases, thereby demonstrating his commitment to a principle espoused by many modern artists – that art should be integrated into everyday life. But his concept of decoration involved another dimension, which he summed up in the following statement: 'Expression and decoration are one and the same thing.' The ornamental motifs of *Dish with Floral Decoration* (top), *Plate with Child's Head and Flowers* (above), and *Plate with Nude Figure* (left) are emblematic of the flowers, faces and nudes that resurface throughout his oeuvre.

Left: Matisse, his wife and Marguerite in front of several works in progress in the Collioure studio in the summer of 1907. Exhibited at the 1908 Salon d'Automne as part of the first retrospective of Matisse's sculpture, *Two Women* (1907, below) combines the way pairs of figures are treated in African art and classical sculpture.

On the grand scale

For Matisse, the art season ended in 1907 as it had the previous spring, with the closing of the Salon des Indépendants (where *Blue Nude: Memory of Biskra* was on view) and his departure for Collioure.

The peaceful landscapes from the summer of 1906 (*Nude in a Wood, Pastoral*) are reminiscent of *Le Bonheur de Vivre*, only now the human figures are all but lost amid the exuberant vegetation. In 1907 Matisse's priorities shifted markedly. The evanescent couples of *Le Bonheur de Vivre* gave way to the sturdily built *Two Women*. The ill-defined, loosely brushed grotto of *Pastoral* was replaced by the crisply delineated abstract cliff of *Brook with Aloes*.

He toned down the colours of his vibrant Neo-Impressionist palette to a more subdued key. The Cézannesque offensive that had begun with *Self-Portrait Sculpting* (1906) and expanded early that year with *Blue Nude* gathered momentum shortly after his arrival in Collioure with a towering composition entitled *Le Luxe (II)* (1907–8).

Above: *Study for 'Le Luxe (I)'* (1907). Left: *Le Luxe (II)* (1907–8).

Revisiting *Le Bonheur de Vivre* on a more monumental scale, the two versions of *Le Luxe* are decorative interpretations of Cézanne's *Le Berger Amoureux* filtered through Gauguin and Puvis de Chavannes. The pastoral scene, set against a bay similar to that of Saint-Tropez, features a Venus-like pagan figure, a crouching votary and a third woman with a bouquet. The scene's idyllic mood is undisturbed by sexual enigma. The ornamental women Matisse created for this paradisiacal setting exude both refinement and Arcadian simplicity.

Undreamed-of splendour

The 1906 Salon d'Automne had confirmed Matisse's pivotal role among 'advanced' artists. Apollinaire's first article on Matisse (12 October 1907) described him as 'the Fauve of Fauves…whose [paintings] no one dared turn down' – which didn't prevent

one of his submissions from being rejected anyway. The poet also interviewed the painter for the journal *La Phalange*. The 'monster' Apollinaire expected to meet turned out to be a 'subtle innovator...an artist in whom are combined France's tenderest qualities: the force of her simplicity and the mellowness of her light'. His appreciation of Matisse as a distinctively French artist included the statement that 'if the goal is to create, there must be an order of which instinct is the measure'.

By late 1907 Matisse's work showed conflicting tendencies: on the one hand, a decorative style with unmodulated fields of brilliant colour; on the other, a virtually achromatic, volumetric approach. This was the dividing line around which his relationship with Picasso was to evolve.

Matisse may or may not have seen Picasso's landmark Cubist painting, *Les Demoiselles d'Avignon* (1906–7), but Picasso's interest was certainly aroused by *Le Bonheur de*

Vivre and *Blue Nude*. Before starting his sculpture *Two Women* (1907), Matisse had probably admired the two monumental nudes Picasso had just created.

By the same token, Matisse's *Bathers with a Tortoise* and *Game of Bowls* (both 1908) were responses to the monumental style Picasso had spent the previous year exploring. Another by-product of this phase of the Matisse-Picasso dialogue, *Standing Nude* (1906–7), closely resembles a figure in *Les Demoiselles d'Avignon*. Matisse's *Boy with a Butterfly Net* (1907) is a classicizing response to the one Picasso had done of the same subject in 1906.

But if Matisse sought fresh inspiration in existing images, the impetus came not so much from increased contact with outside sources as remembered experience. Earlier that year, for example, after repeated unsuccessful attempts to complete a woman's portrait, Matisse headed back to the Louvre to see a Veronese portrait (*Belle Nani*) whose pose and attire reminded him of his model's. As he later did in *Harmony in Red/La Desserte*,

The gigantic decorative figures featured in *Game of Bowls* (1908, opposite above) and *Bathers with a Tortoise* (1908, above) hark back to Cézanne's *Three Bathers* (1879–82). Matisse countered Picasso's Cézanne-inspired Cubism with these monumental compositions that stress harmonious, expressive body movement. He executed rapid line drawings like *Standing Nude* (1907–8, opposite below) 'in which forceful [expression] must take precedence over any and all disproportion'.

he proceeded to change the entire complexion of his painting. 'It's taken on undreamed-of splendour,' he declared as he finished it.

'I have always sought to be understood'

Through the initiative of Sarah Stein (whose husband, Michael Stein, provided financial backing), a young German artist named Hans Purrmann, and the American painter Patrick Henry Bruce, Matisse began to teach in early 1908 at the Couvent des Oiseaux. When the Académie Matisse expanded to nearly fifty students, it moved to the former Couvent du Sacré-Coeur, Boulevard des Invalides. Max Weber, Greta and Oscar Moll, and artists from Scandinavia and central Europe numbered among his students.

The curriculum was nothing if not traditional – drawing from classical sculpture and live models,

Above: Michael and Sarah Stein, Matisse, Allan Stein and Hans Purrmann in the Steins' Paris apartment (c. 1907). Below: Matisse (centre) among his students (1909–10). Right: red transformed the scene depicted in *Harmony in Red/La Desserte* (1908) into an exploration of the unlimited decorative potential of colour.

still life, sculpture – but Matisse taught that one method was as good as another. His in-depth lessons in conventional approaches to expression ('the area occupied by the bodies, the spaces around them, the proportions') were supplemented by equally detailed instruction in composition ('the art of making a decorative arrangement of the elements a painter draws upon in order to express his feelings'). He taught that colour theory should be based on powerful relations of contrast and affinity; that the best way to avoid arbitrary dispersal was never to allow anything to come between colour and sensation; and that a few essential lines were all an artist needed to express the 'deep gravity' of the human figure. He interspersed technical pointers with comments about art ('a soothing, calming influence on the mind'), the difference between working from nature and from the imagination, rules ('they have no existence outside individuals'), and the contemporary art scene.

Dance and music

Sergey Ivanovich Shchukin started buying Matisse's work on a regular basis in 1906; another Russian collector and a friend of Shchukin's, Ivan Morosov, followed suit soon afterwards. In 1908 Shchukin purchased *Harmony in Red*, which was painted that year.

Shchukin was so pleased with his latest purchase that he approached Matisse about doing a decorative painting on the dance, a fashionable subject. Matisse borrowed the circle of dancers from *Le Bonheur de Vivre* – the ones so far upstage they look like an afterthought – and immediately got to work. In a single burst of inspiration, he finished an oil sketch, *Dance (I)*, that combined the freshness of a colossal watercolour with unprecedented energy and decisiveness. It was all Shchukin needed to give

● I did sculpture as a complementary study [to painting], ● Matisse later said. His investigation of the human foot included modelling (1909, below) to help him convey the intensely energetic bounding movement of the figures in *Dance (I)*.

Matisse his approval to complete the commission. The canvas that soon followed, *Dance (II)*, shifted the colouring of the first version to a more violent key, whipped its cavorting dancers into a rapturous outburst more primal and purposeful than in the oil sketch, and set the whole composition on a monumental scale. The dance movements themselves were not inspired by the barely perceptible carmagnole in *Le Bonheur de Vivre* or by what Matisse remembered about the sardanas he had witnessed in the south of France, but by the farandole he had seen at a Paris cabaret.

On 31 March 1909 Shchukin wrote: 'I find your *Dance* panel so noble that I have made up my mind to brave bourgeois public opinion here and hang a subject with nudes on my staircase. At the same time, I'll need another panel, possibly on the subject of music.' Matisse acquiesced at once with an equally large composition with figures making music. A decorative reimagining of Manet's *The Old Musician, Music* (1909–10) raised the chromatic harmony of *Dance (I)* to an even higher pitch that resonates like the richly textured vibrato of a violin.

'No, it's not the wall that suggested the theme [of *Dance*],' Matisse said during a 1951 interview. 'It's that I am particularly fond of the dance and can see more through dance: expressive movement, rhythmic movement, music that I like. That dance was in me.' Matisse made an oil sketch – *Dance (I)*, above – in March 1909, followed by a more intensively worked second version (spring 1910). Overleaf: *Music* (1909–10).

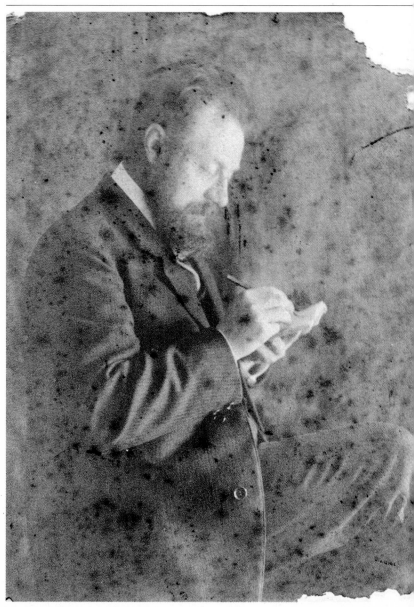

Between the autumn of 1908, when Matisse began *Conversation,* and 1912, the year he finished it, the colour blue flooded his painting, pushing it across another decorative threshold. But his studio was more than just a setting or backdrop for the transcendent dialogue we call art. It was a place of solitude, action and contemplation. It was a place of singular colour.

CHAPTER 4
THE GREAT INDOORS

Opposite: Matisse drawing in a pocket sketchbook in Munich, 1908. Right: *Jeannette (IV)* (1910–1), a sculpture portrait of the same Jeanne Vaderin who sat for *Girl with Tulips* (p. 67), is the penultimate state of a tulip-woman with a stalklike nose and bulbous bunches of hair.

Left: the studio at Issy-les-Moulineaux, 1911, where Matisse painted *Still Life with Geraniums* (below left). On the wall can be seen *Interior with Aubergines* (1911), *Large Nude* (destroyed soon thereafter), Corsican landscapes and other works.

A building that had formerly housed the religious community of Sacré-Coeur had been the Matisse family home since 1908. From its windows they could see the gardens of the Hôtel Biron, now the Rodin Museum, where Rodin maintained one of his studios at the time; its roster of tenants also included the dancer Isadora Duncan.

In the summer of 1909, the convent was sold, and the family moved into a residence they first leased and later bought in Issy-les-Moulineaux, on the outskirts of Paris. The house, which had a solidly middle-class look, opened out on to a large garden. The artist immediately had a wooden studio built near the backyard ornamental pool and greenhouse and filled the house with his collection of paintings, carpets, textiles and *objets d'art.*

Blossoms and models

'Here is my garden,' Matisse told the Danish painter and art historian Ernst Goldschmidt during a 1911 interview. 'This is where I most like to be, after Collioure. Isn't this flower bed more beautiful than the loveliest antique Persian carpet? Look at those colours, how you can tell each of them apart and yet how they blend together.' Garden and painting, equally resplendent, came together. One of the earliest pictures from the Issy period, *Still Life with 'Dance',* combines foreground flowers with the ring of dancers Matisse was then painting for Shchukin.

Similarly, in early 1910, his portrait of a young woman, Jeanne Vaderin, who was convalescing in Issy, places the model behind some tulips that are about to burst open. In the five *Jeannette* busts for which Vaderin also sat, a human face gradually turned into a cluster of bulbous, plantlike masses, a figurative burgeoning and efflorescence. A comparable transposition resulted in the head-turned-blossom that Matisse was to model on his return from Tahiti years later.

Matisse's other sculpture from this period echoes the use of the female body as a plantlike growth issuing from the earth,

In *Girl with Tulips* (*Jeanne Vaderin*) (1910, above), Matisse coupled a portrait of a convalescent with some tulips that are about to burst into bloom. Like the *Jeannette* sculptures, it states the metaphorical link between the natural energy of plant life and the body's innate, organic capacity for healing. The tulips serve as lifelines, infusing the model with renewed vitality.

Left: Matisse at work on *Still Life with 'Dance'* in 1909.

now winding slowly upwards (*La Serpentine*), now thrusting straight into the air like a mighty tree (*The Back* series).

The revelation of the Orient

Shortly after the 1910 Salon d'Automne opened on 1 October, Matisse and Marquet, joined en route by Hans Purrmann, left for Munich to see an exhibition of Islamic art just before it was due to close. Orientalism had long been a familiar part of the European art scene. Matisse had visited Islamic art exhibitions as far back as 1903, and he ranked the Louvre's collections of Islamic ceramics among 'the most remarkable on earth'.

But never before had so many specimens of Islamic art been brought together in one place. Photographs of the exhibition reveal a sumptuous array of overlapping carpets spread out on the floor, lavish textiles and fine embroidery, as well as ceramics, enamelwork and metalwork culled from European and Middle Eastern collections. This stupendous bazaar elicited an enthusiastic response from the trio of friends.

As Matisse devoured everything from miniatures to carpets, he became conscious of a new kind of pictorial space: streaked with arabesques – and other ornaments – or inscriptions, a world apart from the 'cramped space' to which realistically observed motifs were confined. Here was an elusive space, where edges did not cut off a work of art from the mundane reality beyond it, where a profusion of arabesques, ornamental borders and overlapping patterns contributed to a feeling of Edenic immensity. This experience was to have a decisive effect on his work.

When Matisse returned to Paris, not only were critics still railing against *Dance (II)* and *Music*, but Shchukin was starting to waver in his commitment to purchase them. Then Matisse learned that his father had died.

In 1910–1, when Matisse painted *Seville Still Life* (top) and *Spanish Still Life* (above) in his rented studio in Seville, the lavish array of carpets and hangings he had seen in the exhibition of Islamic art in Munich was still fresh in his mind. The real-life blossoms are all but lost in a world of artificiality. Overwhelmed by the floral patterns rippling across the fabrics, the bouquets in the painting are emblems of its decorative vitality and emotion-laden message. The red of the flowers is splashed across the walls.

Matisse was therefore under considerable stress when he set out, unaccompanied, for Spain in November. He looked forward to seeing Islamic ceramics in their natural habitat. After stopping in Madrid, he travelled to Cordova, Seville and Granada, plagued by insomnia. In the two still lifes he brought back from this trip, a field of deep red serves as a backdrop for spiralling decorative fabric patterns.

The Manila Shawl (1911) marked the transition from the depiction of real-life geraniums to the contagious repetition of floral patterns, from the red of petals to the red of burning passions.

A pivotal object lesson in Matisse's aesthetics, *Conversation* (1908–12) has occasioned an astonishing amount of critical comment. Pierre Schneider contends that it transforms a scene from everyday life (Matisse and his wife quarrelling) into a Byzantine icon dominated by the 'central purity' of the window. In his view, it is 'a kind of annunciation and ultimately an epiphany of painting'. The art historian Jack Flam suggests that its composition is 'closely based on the ancient stele of Hammurabi' in the Louvre and that the subject is in fact the monologue of the modern painter. The balcony grillwork spells out 'NON', aimed, he argues, not only at the married couple in the picture but at the observer, cut off from the scene by the picture's purely optical limits. The one point on which these readings agree is that *Conversation* is representative of Matisse's oeuvre as a whole. We know that its companion piece, *Harmony in Red/La Desserte*, began as a blue painting, and the sensual red of *Conversation* was covered over with an abstract blue. Colour never lost its capacity to reveal the painter's secret feelings symbolically.

The symphonic interiors

After Matisse returned to Issy in early 1911, a carpet, a folding screen, and a piece of cloth found their way into *The Pink Studio*, the first of four so-called symphonic interiors painted that year. The palpable presence of the patterned textiles contrasts with the evanescent studio setting, as if decorativeness had begun to empty naturalistic space of everything realistic (despite the inclusion of Matisse's own sculpture in the painting).

Soon after completing *The Pink Studio* that spring, he began work on the next great interior, *The Painter's Family*. Now floral motifs spread across the entire picture surface, turning its human subjects into the adjuncts of a commanding decor. It is they who are the painting's symbolic correlatives. In this first-ever depiction of Matisse's immediate family, the subjects are as detached from one another as the pieces on the chessboard that has riveted the gaze of his identically dressed sons.

'This all or nothing at all is wearing me down,' Matisse wrote on 26 May 1911, referring to *The Painter's Family* (1911, opposite). If a struggle took place, the untroubled, profusely patterned family gathering gives no inkling of it. Pierre and Jean are playing chess, Mme Matisse is embroidering, and Marguerite is standing with a book in her hand.

Left: a 1911 postcard from Matisse with a sketch of the painting.

The family's role, Matisse acknowledged a few years later, was 'purely visual', its purpose to coordinate a ubiquitously, suffocatingly decorative room.

The third member of this quartet of paintings, *Interior with Aubergines*, painted at Collioure that summer, makes use of what André Chastel has called the 'Velázquez effect' (a reference to his fascination with light and reflection); this adds yet another

Below: at Collioure, 1911. Left to right: Mme Matisse, Matisse, a servant, Olga Merson, Marguerite, the painter Albert Huyot and Mme Matisse's father, M. Parayre.

level of complexity to Matisse's treatment of space. Deriving its enigmatic quality from an interplay of a series of frames and mirrors, this work is a declaration of both the bewildering multiplicity of space and the painter's supreme authority in manipulating it. By contrast, the two previous interiors bring out the contemplative side of ornamental art through what might be called a 'Vermeer effect' – luminous colours used in scenes of profound serenity.

The last of the symphonic interiors, *The Red Studio*, painted later that year, shifts the emphasis away from decorativeness and its sub-themes. Matisse turned his studio into a place 'in the mind of the observer', where the only things that stand out against the field of red are his own luminous works of art. The Fauvist landscapes were splashed with red. In his mind's eye, he pictured his career to that point through a red filter.

Interlude in Moscow

In late October 1911, soon after completing *The Red Studio*, Matisse accepted Shchukin's invitation to accompany him on a trip to Moscow by way of St Petersburg. On 5 November Shchukin welcomed him into his house, which boasted a collection of Cézannes, Monets, Gauguins – and twenty-five Matisses. The

Sergey Shchukin (above left), owned thirty-seven of Matisse's paintings when this photograph of the 'Matisse room' in his house (left) was taken around 1914.

presence in Moscow of the first and most famous French painter ever to visit Russia did not go unnoticed: the press trailed him everywhere he went. But the success of his work did not prevent the openly hostile Russian avant-garde from dismissing it as old hat. On 22 November, in 'appalling' weather, Matisse left Moscow, bent on heading back south as soon as possible 'in search of sun'.

L ike *Harmony in Red, The Red Studio* (1911) was originally a pale blue interior with yellow ochre highlights.

'The sublime come to life'

On 29 January 1912 the painter was on the bridge of the *Ridjani*, the ship that was taking him and his wife to Tangier. 'Splendid weather,' he wrote to Marguerite, who had stayed behind in Paris. Marquet had spent part of the previous summer in Morocco and had persuaded his old friend to winter there. He even intimated that he would join him (but never did, despite Matisse's repeated entreaties). When

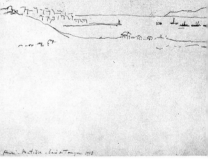

T op: Matisse surveying the Bay of Tangier in 1912. He sketched it in 1913 (above and detail, below).

the Matisses checked into the Hôtel Villa de France, it was raining heavily.

'I have been in Tangier for a month,' he wrote to a friend on 1 March. 'After raining for two solid weeks, as I have never seen it rain before, the weather has turned fair, charming, delightfully soft.' 'What mellow light,' he enthused to a friend the same day. 'Not at all like the Riviera, and the vegetation as exuberant as Normandy's, but oh, so decorative! How utterly new this all is, how difficult to convey with blue, red, yellow and green.'

A similar feeling of giddiness had overcome Eugène Delacroix years earlier, in 1832, as he marvelled not just at the dazzling colours of Tangier but also at examples of 'the sublime come to life': the 'positively antique' costumes, the dark-blue or canary-yellow caftans, the 'amaranth-coloured' and 'scarlet' fabrics, the red bridles and, above all, a sea that was 'dark greenish blue like a fig', and the 'hellish sun' blazing overhead.

Confined to the hotel by the weather, Matisse painted a bouquet of blue irises (*Vase of Irises*) in his room. He spent the next few days drawing the Bay of Tangier under persistently threatening skies. As they cleared, a deep blue spread across *Landscape Viewed from a Window*. *Basket of Oranges* signalled the return of sunny weather.

Matisse described the grounds of the villa where he painted *Park at Tangier/Moroccan Landscape*, the first of three Moroccan garden pictures (1912, above), as 'immense, with meadows as far as the eye could see. I was enraptured by the big trees towering overhead, while the rich acanthuses below were so sumptuous they seemed to vie for my attention'.

Window on Morocco

Matisse spent many work sessions registering his impressions of a Tangier park and followed up with two freer, more spontaneous variations on the garden theme. He later said that he painted one of them, *The Palm*, in 'a burst of spontaneous creation, like a flame'.

Matisse was back in France by 19 April. The blue of *Landscape Viewed from a Window* now flooded across *Conversation*, which he had begun in 1908. In late September he returned to Tangier to work on a pair of landscapes Ivan Morosov had commissioned. But he found that the soft greens and greenish blues of Moroccan springtime had been replaced by the 'lion-skin' ochres of drought. Bereft of the subjects that had enraptured him earlier that year, Matisse went horse riding and read. He was joined by his friend Charles Camoin and his wife at the end of November.

As another 'window on Morocco', *The Casbah Gate*, took shape that winter, the almond green and pinkish

The Casbah Gate and *Landscape Viewed from a Window* (both 1912–3, below left and right) fulfilled a commission Matisse received from Ivan Morosov. The view through his window became known as 'the blue landscape'. During his second trip to Tangier, Matisse covered the soft green and pink tonalities of the original painting with a delightful blue, which then overran his depiction of the gate above the casbah.

Matisse painted the girl portrayed in *Zorah Seated* (1912, left) several times during his two stays in Tangier. Did he intend for this large signed oil drawing to be a part of the so-called Moroccan Triptych, comprising *On the Terrace* (1912–3, above) and the two paintings on the opposite page? He may have started it independently in case Zorah's brothers should decide to deprive him of his model. After a first sitting during which he 'more or less spontaneously' captured his model in a state of 'uninterrupted reverie', Matisse transformed the girl into an image reminiscent of the Virgin as depicted in Russian icons.

ochre of the initial sketch turned a delicate blue, and the gate swelled like burgeoning flower bulb. This painting, *Landscape Viewed from a Window*, and *On the Terrace* ultimately comprised a triptych wholly given over to the blue tonalities earlier Romantic artists had found so compelling. Indoor scenes featuring flowers and caftan-clad Riffians (northern African Berbers) captured the remembered exuberance and wildness of spring. Matisse's second trip to Morocco ended in mid-February 1913 with the decorative *Moroccan Café*, a luminous, trancelike suspension of space and time that conveys to perfection the 'utter calm' the artist had found in Tangier.

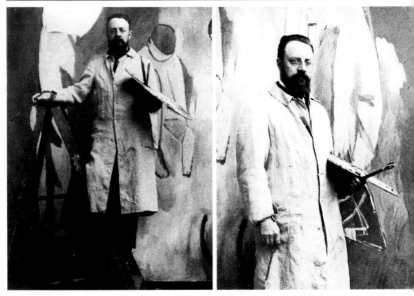

The rite of spring

Memories of Tangier suffuse the paintings Matisse created in the spring of 1913, after his return to Issy-les-Moulineaux (by way of Marseilles and Corsica). A field of deep blue blanketed the almond green of *Flowers and Ceramic Plate* and *The Blue Window*. Blue acted as a Cézannesque nimbus, a veil interposed between the geometric forms of Cubism and the Morocco Matisse saw in his mind's eye. For a while longer, blue brought together his subjective vision of the East and the objective world of framed still lifes and landscapes.

That summer he reworked *The Back (I)* (1908–9) into a more architectural relief sculpture and returned to his huge unfinished painting of women bathing by a waterfall, a sketch of which he had submitted to Shchukin in the spring of 1909 as a prospective sequel to *Dance (II)* and *Music*.

While the First World War raged, *Goldfish and Palette* (1914, below) declared the importance of a painter's work as an active, constructive endeavour.

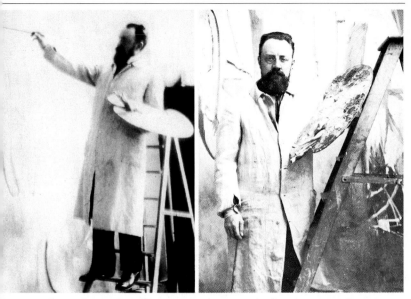

Later known as *Bathers by a River* (1909–16, overleaf), this scene originally featured a kind of Moroccan garden with upright bands of vermilion, blue and green, as though Matisse were transposing on to canvas the monumental feel of *The Back* sculptures.

But there is a noticeable difference between the mood in this painting and in the earlier decorative works. This was no time for celebrations of life and vernal rings of dancers, but instead for the anxieties induced by impending war. Its original colours – the vibrant tones used in *Dance* and *Music* – were replaced by bands of green, black, white and grey.

It was in this atmosphere of foreboding that Matisse painted his last portrait of his wife. In it her face has given way to the abstract features of an African mask. The 'happy times in Morocco' were a distant memory.

He began another large decorative painting, *The Moroccans*, an abstract composition built up from luminous, blocklike patches of black, grey and ochre – pictorial equivalents of the blocks of sound in Igor Stravinsky's *The Rite of Spring* (1913).

In May 1913 the photographer Alvin Langdon Coburn captured Matisse in his Issy-les-Moulineaux studio working on *Bathers by a River*, a huge composition (overleaf) that he began in 1909 but was not to finish until the autumn of 1916. Although its architectonic forms seem to be a nod to Cubism and Picasso's *Les Demoiselles d'Avignon,* the emphasis is clearly on decorative primitivism. The influence of Puvis de Chavannes and Rodin can also be seen in these towering Cézannesque bathers who do not seem in the least bit flustered by an intruding snake.

Before the German invasion of France, Matisse painted the cathedral of Notre-Dame as though it were a goldfish bowl, a fragile, transparent bulwark against the approaching conflict.

Substance and remembrance

When Germany declared war on France on 3 August 1914, Matisse had just finished a series of portraits that included a drawing of Mabel Warren, *Woman on a High Stool (Germaine Raynal)* and the *Portrait of Mlle Yvonne Landsberg*. Repeatedly repainted over a long period of time, this canvas, like the *Jeannette* sculptures, is a visual metaphor of a young woman as a blossoming bud, emanating a series of expanding curves around the model. That spring Matisse had noticed an article on the possibility of photographing a person's soul as it leaves the body at the moment of death – precisely the kind of radiation the ghostly outlines in the uniformly purplish grey backdrop of the Landsberg portrait seem to register.

During this period, the painter was particularly taken with the philosophy of Henri Bergson (whose dualistic world view postulated the life force and the resistance of the world against that force); he held many discussions with the philosopher Matthew Stewart Prichard on Bergson's thinking. Matisse was not only in contact with the Cubist artists Juan Gris, Albert Gleizes, and Jean Metzinger – whose abstract style fragmented structure and space – but also saw a great deal of the artist Gino Severini, who was about to break away from Futurism, with its focus on dynamism and mechanistic energy, to espouse a classicizing idiom rooted in early Italian art. Matisse went to see exhibitions of work by the modernist German groups Die Brücke and Der Blaue Reiter and was in touch with other intellectuals and artists.

In 1914 Matisse saw more of Picasso and struck up a friendship with Juan Gris (below, photographed with his wife, Josette Gris).

Bottom: Germaine Raynal, the wife of the art critic Maurice Raynal, sat for *Woman on a High Stool* early in 1914.

'When the first sitting was over,' Albert Landsberg later recalled, referring to *Portrait of Mlle Yvonne Landsberg* (1914, left) – which was preceded by a portrait etching (above) – 'the oil portrait was a highly recognizable likeness of the model, but it became increasingly abstract.... At every [subsequent] sitting, the portrait looked less like my sister physically, but I dare say more like her spiritually. The colours were superb from the first: steel blue, steel grey, black, orange and white where the canvas showed through those mysterious white lines that cut into the surface'. Matisse later said that the lines were 'lines of construction I put around the figure in order to give it greater amplitude in space'.

Matisse and Marquet met Marcel Sembat, the deputy and then minister of public works, to discuss enlisting. 'Derain, Braque, Camoin and Puy are at the front, risking their necks.... We're sick and tired of staying behind. How can we serve our country?,' they asked. Sembat turned them down with this forthright reply: 'By continuing to paint as well as you do.'

Black over almond green

Bohain-en-Vermandois was trapped behind enemy lines soon after the German offensive began. Matisse's brother, a reserve officer, was held hostage in Heidelberg. His letters told of his deep distress, the endless waiting, the lack of news from his family. After the newspapers announced on 26 August that the retreating French army extended 'from the Somme to the Vosges' – meaning that the roads to Paris and the Channel lay open to the Germans – Matisse and his family left Issy-les-Moulineaux and set off, first for Toulouse.

Then Matisse, his wife and Marquet reached Collioure on 10 September. Juan Gris was already there, and he and Matisse had heated discussions about painting. They called on the sculptor Manolo in nearby Ceret. As he had done in Brittany in 1897, Matisse painted a French window, only this time in the almond green of Tangier, with a swathe of black where light ought to be.

When he returned to Paris that November, he did a series of etchings to benefit the civilian prisoners of Bohain. A 1917 article on the war and these prints praised them for their French sources (Ingres, Rodin), purity of line and patriotic motivation. Matisse also saw collectors on Gris' behalf and assumed responsibility for Derain's business dealings.

The studio Matisse had rented in January 1914 was on the fourth floor of 19, Quai Saint-Michel, below Marquet, who had taken over his old studio. 'My work goes on,' Matisse wrote to Camoin.

The art critic Félix Fénéon (above, depicted by the Swiss artist Félix Vallotton) was a longtime supporter of Matisse. It is to his credit that Matisse was offered a contract with the Bernheim-Jeune gallery in September 1909.

Left: *Greta Prozor Leaning on the Back of a Chair* (1916).

'We are emerging from the Realist movement,' Matisse said in 1909. 'It has garnered some raw materials. They are there. We must now begin the enormous job of organization.' The importance Cubism had assumed in Matisse's eyes is clear in *Still Life after Jan Davidsz. de Heem's 'La Desserte'* (1915), opposite below), painted after his 1893 copy of the Dutch original. Opposite above: a 1915 preparatory drawing.

'I know what I know, only better.'
While painting *Goldfish and Palette*
in the autumn of 1914, he borrowed
a small Seurat canvas that was 'more
intense, more crisply delineated, more
colourful' than the one already on his
wall. Nearby were pinned a
photograph of Delacroix's *Jacob
Wrestling with the Angel* and a
lithograph after a Cézanne still life
of fruit and leaves that he had
recently done for the Bernheim-Jeune
gallery, which represented him for
many years.

On 22 November 1915, he finished a
huge variation on a still life after de
Heem 'according to methods of
modern construction'; a collector

Distraught after Braque and Derain left for the front, Picasso found refuge in tradition: *The Painter and his Model* (above) dates from 1914. In *The Painter in his Studio* (1916, left), however, Matisse pressed ahead with the simplification of form he had begun to explore two years earlier. The emotionally charged dialogue between the artist and his models continued despite the war. To be sure, the angles have stiffened, and the cramped room, with its interrupted view and confining ceiling, has been partitioned into contrasting sectors. But the focal point remains the painter at work, however cut off from the theatre of operations he may be.

immediately snapped it up. 'I saw a recent Picasso at [this collector's place],' Matisse wrote to Derain, 'a harlequin done in a new style, without collages, using nothing but paint. Are you familiar with it?'

The painting lesson

Matisse returned to *The Moroccans* while still at work on *Bathers by a River*, an updated version of a painting by the Realist Gustave Courbet. Courbet's *The Painter's Studio* (1855), the source of Picasso's unfinished, naturalistic *The Painter and his Model* (1914), also made its presence felt in Matisse's variation on the studio theme in the winter of 1916–7. Matisse responded to Picasso's melancholy artist (who does not paint) with an artist at work, an anonymous mediator between the principal combatants of his struggle as a painter: model, window, mirror, canvas.

Matisse featured images of his bronze *Decorative Figure* (1908) and *Woman on a High Stool* (1914) in the monumental *Piano Lesson* (late summer 1916) in order to articulate, if not reconcile, the conflicting aspirations of a solitary creator who finds himself torn between polar opposites.

The following summer, with Europe engulfed in all-out war and both troops and civilians showing signs of weariness, Matisse seemed to take up this theme in *The Music Lesson*. In terms of subject matter, however, the two paintings are worlds apart. The lone artist at odds with his career has been replaced by the painter's loved ones, whom he gathered together one last time to create the heartening image associated with family life during that 'year of gloom'.

Matisse's younger son, Pierre, did not wait to be called up and was assigned to the tank corps. Jean was conscripted into the air force ground staff. As one critic has suggested, the artist's ruthless self-centredness had, at least in one painting, finally deferred to the moral imperatives of family and patriotism.

In *Piano Lesson* (1916, above), Matisse reminds us that the most urgent task facing any artist – a young beginner (like his son Pierre, shown seated at the piano) or an old-timer – is to play his part well.

'Everything was fake, absurd, amazing, delightful,' Matisse later said, remembering the hotel room in Nice that became his haven in late 1917. The pervasive decorativeness that its sets and props inspired would dominate his work during his Nice period until his trip to the South Seas intervened.

CHAPTER 5

'THE OBJECTS OF MY REVERIE'

Henriette Darricarrère was more than an anonymous model depicted as an object in a pictorial field, as in *Decorative Figure on an Ornamental Ground* (1925–6, opposite). A painter and musician herself, she was Matisse's partner in a theatre of painting (with the artist in his apartment in 1921, right) and played a unique role within his family of models.

'In those trying times,' Matisse recalled, 'I would wait for bulletins and the mail. I was no longer able to immerse myself in a picture that would have required too much time to give substance to my feelings. I painted landscapes.'

He would load all of his 'paraphernalia' into his new car, a Renault 11 that could easily take him to the nearby woods, and drive off to paint outdoors. His rekindled interest in landscapes was no accident. The same impulse to investigate the French countryside had motivated Monet (whom Matisse later visited at his home in Giverny) and Corot. In a few months' time, it would also lead him to Renoir's villa on the French Riviera.

After 1914 Matisse never passed up a chance to head south, although he did not go as far afield as Tangier.

Matisse at work on *Self-Portrait* (1918).

In December 1915 Marquet and he travelled to Marseilles, on the Mediterranean coast. Nothing ever came of a plan to return the next month and look for a studio. But he did go back in late October 1917, painted two portraits of the critic and collector Georges Besson in his hotel room, and worked on a drawing of trees at L'Estaque, to the west.

A room with a view

Matisse contracted bronchitis while working outdoors in windy weather, so he left Marseilles to recuperate in Nice, a resort city

By uprooting himself and distancing himself from his family, Matisse recaptured the intimacy that comes with solitude. In *Self-Portrait* (1918, left), the artist's thumb and a paintbrush, sticking up like an oversized index finger, symbolize his creative potency.

So what if Matisse's hotel room was cramped? Nice had brilliant light, and that meant more than anything else. A 1912 view of the Bay of Nice (below).

further east, near the Italian border, famous for its mild climate and comfortable hotels. On 20 December 1917 he checked into a cramped room with a sea view in the Hôtel Beau-Rivage. Making the best of a month-long spell of inclement weather, he dashed off a series of interiors reminiscent of summery Impressionistic *pochades*, only using the more scintillating light of Nice, and *Interior with a Violin*, a legacy from the geometric idiom of 1916.

On 31 December he called on Renoir. 'I greatly admired him,' he later told Picasso, who shared his keen interest in the older artist. 'So I paid him a visit at Les Collettes, his place in Cagnes. He gave me a cordial reception.' When Matisse showed Renoir the canvases he had done since his arrival, the aged painter, despite a 'somewhat disapproving air', complimented him on his deft handling of black. On a subsequent visit, Matisse again showed him his paintings: 'Not bad,' commented Renoir, 'but not enough like Courbet.' 'Oh, Renoir was a marvel!' Matisse declared when the painter died in June 1919. 'I have always thought that no era boasted a nobler,

Matisse once said that *Interior with a Violin* (1917–8, above left) was 'one of my loveliest paintings'.

more heroic story or a more splendid achievement than that of Renoir.' Were it not for the psychological boost his contact with Renoir provided, the atmosphere of Oriental sensuality Matisse had hinted at, but failed to capture, in Marseilles might never have been reawakened.

A painter's props

'I've been detained here by some landscapes…' Matisse notified Camoin on 10 April 1918, 'and I don't expect to head back until I've got something worthwhile out of them, or so I hope.' It was around this time that he decided to remain in Nice and to arrange his personal life according to the demands of his art. He would spend rainy days painting flowers at the studio he rented next door to his hotel from February to April 1918.

'I'm also working at the Ecole des Arts Décoratifs, which is run by Paul Audra, a former student of Moreau's,' he continued. 'I've been drawing *Night* [1524–34] and…modelling it and studying with Michelangelo's *Lorenzo de' Medici.* I hope to instil in

Above: Matisse called on Renoir at Les Collettes, the aged artist's villa at nearby Cagnes-sur-Mer. Matisse is in the centre of the photograph above, with Renoir seated to his left.

Matisse painted *Violinist at the Window* (opposite right) in 1918, but left unfinished *Violinist* (opposite below), a large charcoal drawing on canvas that shows his son Pierre practising the violin.

myself the clear yet complex concept of Michelangelo's construction.'

In May he moved to the Villa des Alliés, not far from a lush park, high above the city. He began the yearly cycle of spending the summer season in Paris and returning to Nice in the autumn, and he was not alone in doing so. Apollinaire mentioned the exodus of painters from Paris in April 1918: 'Matisse is in Nice, Kisling is on the shores of the Mediterranean with Iribe and Signac close by. Juan Gris, Ortiz de Zarate, Modigliani, Van Dongen and Georges Braque have also deserted the capital for the Avignon countryside.'

In November 1918 Matisse took up residence in the Hôtel de la Méditerranée et de la Côte d'Azur, a 'good, old hotel' he liked for its lovely Italianate ceilings, tile floors and louvred shutters that let in light, as he later said, 'from below, like footlights'.

The props of Nice – a parasol, a folding screen, a mirror – inspired groups of pictures organized around the same motif. Matisse replaced Lorette, the model he had used for his recent Parisian canvases, with Antoinette Arnoux, who would be the principal player in his new theatre. Now, something as simple as a plumed hat could lead to 'a whole series of drawings…after a single detail'.

Tea in a French garden

During the summer of 1919, at Issy-les-Moulineaux, Matisse painted a large decorative canvas, *Tea in the Garden*, whose subject and size (140.3 x 211.5 cm) evoke the painting of Monet. Lily, his sheepdog, is scratching her ear while Marguerite dangles a shoe. The place of Madame Matisse, in poor health since the end of the war, has been taken by the model Antoinette. But there is nothing Edenic about this garden of undisguised

●Look at that portrait of a young woman with an ostrich feather in her hat,● Matisse said in 1919, referring to *The Plumed Hat* (1919, above). 'The feather is an ornament, a decorative element, but in addition to that it has body, a lightness you can almost feel, a downy, impalpable softness you can fairly blow on…. I want simultaneously to convey the typical and the individual, a summation of everything I see and feel in front of a subject.'

boredom except for unobtrusive reminders of Biskra's palm trees in the middle ground and of the tall shade trees he painted in Tangier.

In May Félix Fénéon organized Matisse's first show since 1913 at the Bernheim-Jeune gallery in Paris.

Above: *The Moorish Screen* (1921).
Overleaf: *Tea in the Garden* (1919).

Jean Cocteau, for one, was not pleased with what he saw. 'The sun-drenched Fauve has turned into a Bonnard kitten,' he wrote. 'The atmosphere of Bonnard, Vuillard and Marquet pervades the room.'

'I did Impressionist work, directly from nature,' Matisse told the critic Ragnar Hoppe that summer. 'Later I strove for concentration and a more intense expression with line as well as colour, at which point I obviously had to sacrifice other values to some extent: substance, spatial depth, richness of detail. Now I want to bring all this together and I think I'll be able to, in time.'

Igor Stravinsky and Sergey Diaghilev, impresario of the Ballets Russes, approached Matisse about designing the costumes and sets for a three-act ballet based on a lyrical fairy tale, *Le Rossignol* (The Nightingale),

LE CHANT DU ROSSIGOL

which Stravinsky had begun in 1908 and reworked in 1914 as *Le Chant du Rossignol* (The Song of the Nightingale). The idea of an imaginary China, expressed through Stravinsky's evocative orchestral score and Léonide Massine's choreography, appealed to Matisse at once. He accepted the commission. 'I learned that costumes could be conceived of as moving colours,' he wrote in 1913. 'The colours move about, yet must not alter the general effect of the decor.' In September he left for London to work on the project.

But all did not go easily. 'There was a Cubist clique when I was working on *Le Rossignol*,' he told Pierre Courthion. 'All the people who usually had a kind word for me turned their backs on me. All the glory was supposed to go to Manuel da Falla's ballet [*The Three-Cornered Hat*], with sets by Picasso.'

A few days before the premiere of the ballet on 2 February 1920, Matisse's mother died. That summer the artist headed north to Etretat, on the English

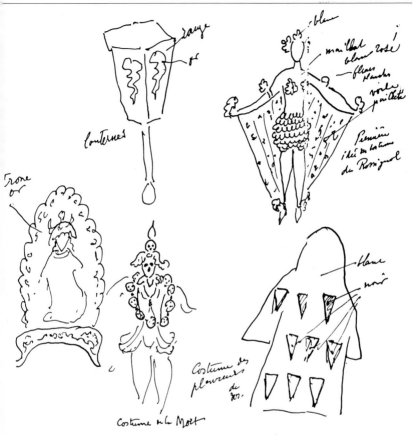

Channel, where Courbet and Monet had painted before him. There were also reminders of Chardin and Manet evident in his paintings of rays and other fish spread out on the sandy shore like so many offerings to his mother and the land of his childhood.

A private theatre

The painter returned to Nice in late September 1920, after the Bernheim-Jeune gallery published *Cinquante Dessins par Henri-Matisse* (Fifty Drawings by Henri Matisse). The first monograph ever devoted to the artist

Matisse's sets (one example, opposite above) and costumes (preparatory sketches, above) for *Le Chant du Rossignol* featured combinations of green, pink, light blue and saffron yellow against a white backdrop. Opposite: Igor Stravinsky (c. 1918, left) and Sergey Diaghilev (1916, right).

Michelangelo's *Night* (above) is one source for Matisse's *Large Seated Nude* (below). An early version of Matisse's monumental sculpture is visible in the foreground of a 1926 photograph (above left) of the artist at work on *Henriette (II)*. Opposite below: *Reclining Nude* (1925).

had appeared a few months earlier. And Bernheim-Jeune went on to publish a second volume on Matisse with essays by several writers that year.

Henriette Darricarrère was now Matisse's model; she continued to sit for him until 1927. In the autumn of 1921 he rented a third-floor apartment facing the sea in the former residence of the historian Comte de Pierlas, at 1, Place Charles-Félix, at one end of Old Nice's market street. Here, amid profusely patterned wallpaper, he set up a 'private little Oriental theatre' (in the words of one writer) complete with flowered fabrics, wall hangings, carpets and enclosed balconies. Matisse would carefully arrange these props to suit each picture's tonality and shift them about to dramatize the odalisques (slaves or concubines in a harem) he painted there until 1930, when he went to Tahiti.

The 1920s were an eventful period for Matisse. There were exhibitions in Paris and abroad; new collectors – notably Albert C. Barnes and Claribel and

Etta Cone – were purchasing his work; Marguerite married the critic Georges Duthuit, a modern scholar of Byzantine art; and Pierre set sail for New York, where he later opened his own gallery. 'Yes,' the artist later said, 'I needed a breather so that I could unwind and forget all my cares, far from Paris. The *Odalisques* were the fruit of a blissful nostalgia, of a beautiful waking dream, of something I experienced during virtually ecstatic days and nights in a spellbinding atmosphere.'

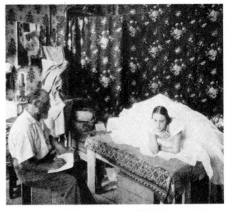

The single most outstanding sculpture of the decade – the largest freestanding sculpture he made – was *Large Seated Nude* (1925–9), an offshoot of the drawings he had done after Michelangelo's *Night* (1524–34) at the Ecole des Arts Décoratifs in Nice. Matisse tried out various dynamic poses against his apartment's decorative surfaces. A foil to his planar stage sets, this volumetric human figure reintroduced the tension that very nearly evaporated in the evanescent light of the early Nice

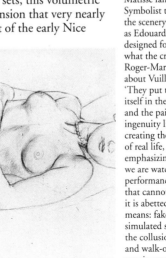

The indolence of Matisse's Nice period pictures was carefully staged. Above: Henriette Darricarrère posing on the raised platform of a theatre that was the decorative equivalent of model and set. Was Matisse familiar with Symbolist theatre and the scenery artists such as Edouard Vuillard had designed for it? Consider what the critic Claude Roger-Marx had to say about Vuillard's sets: 'They put theatricality itself in the limelight, and the painter's ingenuity lies not in creating the illusion of real life, but in emphasizing that what we are watching is a performance, a show that cannot go on unless it is abetted by artificial means: fake lighting, simulated surroundings, the collusion of disguises and walk-ons wearing makeup.'

Matisse drawing Henriette Darricarrère on the mini-proscenium on which he posed so many of his odalisques. He used his many multicoloured, patterned fabric hangings as screens.

Below: *Henriette (II)* (1925–6), second and most classical in a series of three 'expressive heads'.

interiors. 'With the *Odalisques*, I did not repudiate what I had recently acquired,' he said. 'I did, however, return to a resonance of depth and allowed some modelling to reappear. I regained possession of a space where air could freely circulate again.'

The summer of 1925 found him on a second trip to Italy (Rome, Naples, Sicily), this time with his wife, Marguerite, and Georges Duthuit. Afterwards, back in Nice, he painted one Michelangelesque odalisque after another.

In the autumn of the following year, he moved to the fourth floor of 1, Place Charles-Félix, a brighter apartment that let in more of the sea and infused a new sense of scale into his pictorial space. Reflected by an unusual false-tile wall covering, the light that poured into this work space lent his canvases a pearly transparency and dissolved the very substance of some

of the nudes who sat for him in the studio. In the unfinished *Woman with a Madras Hat* (1929–31), for example, his model is nothing more than a dematerialized silhouette of white canvas with faintly drawn features. Meanwhile, huge, majestic bouquets of gladiolus and dahlias seemed to beckon Matisse to the outside world, which can be seen peeking through the background window in *The Yellow Dress* (1929–31), a painting he left unfinished when he set sail for Tahiti.

The painter on holiday

One of the main reasons Matisse made his trip to Tahiti in February 1930 was to search for 'a different light', the same quest that had originally brought him to the shores of the Mediterranean. He stated in a 1942 radio interview that he kept coming back to Nice because of the 'silvery

Odalisque with a Turkish Chair (1927–8). 'Look closely at these odalisques,' Matisse once wrote. 'Sunlight floods over them in all its triumphant brilliance.... Now, the Oriental decor of the interiors, the array of hangings and carpets, the sumptuous costumes...ought not to delude us.... There is a great tension brewing, a tension of a specifically pictorial order that arises from the interplay and mutual relations of the various elements.'

clarity of its light, especially during the beautiful month of January'. He had marvelled at the light of Corsica, Collioure and Tangier. The 'very pure, immaterial, crystalline light' he saw during a stopover in New York impressed him almost as much as the light he encountered when he reached the South Pacific (like gazing into 'a deep golden goblet', he later rhapsodized).

The South Seas also held out the promise of the larger space that Matisse was seeking at the time. Arriving in New York on 4 March, he was dumbfounded by what he saw. As he later said, 'I have always been conscious of another space in which the objects of my reverie might evolve. I was seeking something other than real space. Hence my curiosity for the other hemisphere, where things could happen differently.' He visited the Metropolitan Museum of Art and saw 'some extraordinary Monets as well as three Cézannes, works by Degas, Renoir and Courbet, and some questionable Rembrandts'. As America rolled past his train window on his way to California, he was struck by its 'immensity' and its 'blinding' light. Los Angeles was a 'Côte d'Azur on a huge scale', and the gardens there reminded him of Morocco.

Above: Matisse in Manhattan. 'If I weren't so accustomed to standing by my decisions,' he wrote to his wife on 5 March 1930, en route to Tahiti, 'I would go no further than New York, so impressed am I with this new world. It's big and majestic, like the sea.... There's a grandeur of space and order here.... American light is bright, intensely bright.'

Matisse left *The Yellow Dress* (1929–31, opposite) unfinished when he went to the South Pacific but completed it when he got back to Nice. His trip provided the picture with a fresh point of departure.

On 21 March he was aboard the *Tahiti*, drawing terns. 'Surrounded by a crown of gold, ibises, and opaline blue,' the dark-blue sea reminded him of a blue morpho butterfly he had bought in Paris on his return from Ajaccio. 'I shall go to the islands,' he wrote before he left, 'to contemplate night and the light of dawn, which probably have a different density in the tropics.' In Tahiti he was captivated by 'the water of the lagoon, coloured a greyish jade green by the bottom, which lies very close, the branching corals and their variety of soft pastel tones, around which dart schools of little blue fish'. He expected to amass 'many documents which I hope will be of use to me for a long time to come in France'. He met F. W. Murnau while the film director was shooting *Tabu*.

But after the first dazzling day – 'I find everything wonderful: scenery, trees, flowers, people,' including Tuamotu natives he thought looked like sea gods – the 'steambath' proved too much for him. Overwhelming fatigue prevented him from working. 'Dear friend,' he wrote to Pierre Bonnard on 6 June. 'Am taking the boat for Panama in a week. Will be in Nice late July or thereabouts. Good stay, good rest. Saw all sorts of things. Will tell you about it. Spent twenty days on a "coral isle": pure light, pure air, pure colours: diamond, sapphire, emerald, turquoise. Breathtaking fish. Did absolutely nothing, except take bad photos. Stay well, both of you. Will be glad to see France again.' Matisse had returned to France by 31 July.

Back in Nice, he again turned his attention to *The Yellow Dress*, which he later confessed had been on his

Matisse and a friend, Pauline Schile, in Tahiti (1930, left). In 1941 he wrote to Louis Aragon about a 'Tahitian girl with satin skin and soft curly hair and a copper complexion that blends sumptuously with the island's dark greenery'. 'The rich fragrance of frangipani…of blossoming pandanus trees that smell like freshly baked bread, the almost suffocating scent of tuberoses and of the Tahitian flower, the tiari' would linger in the painter's memory for many more years to come.

mind the whole time he was away. Now his real work began. 'Such colours,' he said in 1931 about Tahitian skies, 'cannot bear fruit except in memory, after they have been weighed against our own colours. I expect that some of it will filter into my painting, later on. I am convinced that exactly the same held true for Delacroix with his trip to Morocco. Its colours did not show up in his paintings until ten years later.' Little by little, Tahiti, with its dazzling colours, was to make its presence felt thematically and spatially, gradually suffusing the rest of Matisse's career with its fragrance.

Below: 'the elegant coconut palms with their upswept hair', drawn and photographed by Matisse in 1930.

'Art may be said to imitate nature…by the life that the creative worker infuses into the work of art. The work of art will then appear as fertile and as possessed of the same power to thrill – the same resplendent beauty – as we find in works of nature,' Matisse said in an interview in 1954, the year he died. 'Great love is needed to achieve this effect, a love capable of inspiring and sustaining that patient striving towards truth, that glowing warmth, and that analytic profundity that accompany the birth of any work of art.'

CHAPTER 6
A PERFECT UNITY

Matisse hard at work in his studio at the Hôtel Régina, Nice-Cimiez (1952, opposite). Right: a bunch of flowers in a tobacco jar from a 1948 book that Matisse illustrated.

In 1930, in a departure from his usual routine, Matisse
went back to Nice in August, his memories of Tahiti
gradually encroaching on his world. A sculpture
completed at the end of the summer (*Tiari*) turned
a human head into a Tahitian flower the same way
Jeannette's face had metamorphosed into a tulip two
decades earlier. In September Matisse returned to the
United States to serve on the jury of an international
exhibition of painting at the Carnegie Institute in
Pittsburgh, which had awarded him first prize in its 1927
exhibition. That year's Carnegie prize went to Picasso.

On 28 September Matisse travelled to the Philadelphia
suburb of Merion to see Dr Albert C. Barnes, a collector
he had met after the First World War who had already
acquired many of his paintings. Barnes asked Matisse to
do a mural decoration for the main hall of the private
foundation he had established in 1922 and assured the
artist that he would be given a completely free hand.
Enraptured by all the Picassos, Renoirs and Seurats on
display at the foundation, Matisse could not turn the
commission down.

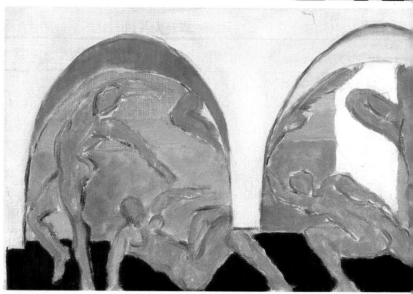

The Barnes Foundation *Dance*

He returned to France and two months later, in Nice, began a series of small studies in pencil and oil. In December he was back in Merion to make a detailed assessment of the challenges posed by the site of his prospective mural. It was to fit under three separate, enormous arches, each above a tall French window.

Matisse rented a cavernous vacant garage in the heart of Nice to use as a studio and in early 1931 began to work on the great mural. The subject – the dance – was a familiar one, which had first appeared in his oeuvre in 1905.

To make revising his work easier, instead of painting, Matisse started

Opposite top: Matisse sketching the early unfinished version of *Dance* in the vacant garage in Nice (1931). The first finished version (centre) was abandoned while Matisse worked on the final mural, which was completed and installed in 1933 in the main hall of the Barnes Foundation. This room already boasted a number of important paintings, including Cézanne's *The Cardplayers,* Renoir's *The Artist's Family* and Seurat's *Models.* Displayed against the light, Matisse's decoration would be visible from two balconies on the opposite side of the room and from the floor of the gallery (where, he commented, 'it will be more felt than seen'). Extremely mindful of these factors, Matisse saw to it that 'the mural would not overwhelm the room but, on the contrary, give the pictures in it breathing space'.

Left: *Study for the Dance Mural* (1930–1), a small, early oil study for the unfinished version, which was rolled up, put away and not rediscovered until 1992.

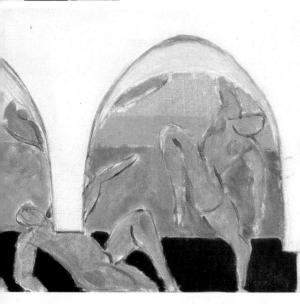

working with pieces of painted-and-cut paper that could be easily pinned and moved about over the canvas. His first finished version had to be set aside because of a mistake in the measurements, though Matisse returned to it after he completed the final mural. By then, the spring of 1933, the original ring of dancers had evolved into a 'battle of love' spread across slanting bands of unmodulated blue, pink and black.

In the final version, Matisse said he had endeavoured to give 'observers a sensation of flight, of elevation, that induces them to disregard the work's actual dimensions, which are far too inadequate as crowning elements for the glazed doors, and to see it in their mind's eye as a sky for the garden visible through the French windows'. The artist attended the installation of the Barnes Foundation *Dance* on 15 May 1933. 'I'm on my way back from Philadelphia,' he wrote to Pierre Bonnard. 'The mural is in place and looks very fine; I feel it has become an integral part of the building. Its very substance has been transformed.'

Themes and variations

In his postcard Matisse added: 'I'm rather tired and will finally take off part of this summer to relax.' Matisse was now in his sixties. The three years he had devoted almost exclusively to the Barnes commission had taken a toll on his health.

From May to October 1935, Matisse composed *Large Reclining Nude/The Pink Nude* by using paper cutouts as 'quantities' of space and colour to balance its components structurally. Over the months, an initial series of naturalistic states based on a live model evolved into the monumentally decorative final version (left). The artist documented the work's evolution in photographs – it went through twenty-odd states before he had finished it. Above: Matisse's assistant Lydia Delectorskaya rubs out the state dated 15 October 1935. The unfinished *Window at Tahiti (I)* is on the wall behind her, and *The Back (IV)* in plaster is in the background.

A series of pen-and-ink drawings from 1935–6, published in *Cahiers d'Art,* features a number of female nudes leaning back and reflected in a mirror in which Matisse's reflected image can be seen. This process of replication confirms the presence of both painter and model, the latter displayed not only within the drawing but as part of an interplay of drawings within a drawing, a nesting of images that acts as a unifying force. Image and reflected image interpenetrate by means of a mirror and the motionless mediation of the painter himself. Left: *Artist and Model Reflected in a Mirror* (1937), a late addition to the series.

After taking the summer off, Matisse returned to Nice in September and to the version of the Barnes mural that he had had to set aside. He also painted *Woman in a White Dress* and *Interior with a Dog.*

One new passion was illustrated books. While at work on the *Dance* mural, he had done illustrations for his first such book, the publisher Albert Skira's edition of the poems of Stéphane Mallarmé. His overriding concern, he said, was 'to balance the comparatively black page with the type against the comparatively white page with the etching'.

In 1934 Matisse began work on illustrations for an American edition of James Joyce's *Ulysses*. The episodes from Homer's *Odyssey* that inspired his etchings for the novel were to prove a rich source of thematic material in much of his future work.

Still recovering from the strain of the Barnes commission, though, Matisse did not produce much work until 1935. In fact, he had done very little easel painting over the past few years. Was he having second thoughts about the validity of painting, which Bonnard dejectedly referred to as an 'outdated passion'?

'I believe that one day easel painting will cease to

‘*Nymph in the Forest/ La Verdure* (above) was initially conceived as a design for a tapestry,’ noted Lydia Delectorskaya. 'Its original subject was an etching for the 1931 Mallarmé poetry book, reversed and without figures.'

Opposite below: *Nymph and Faun with Pipes* (1940–3).

Exemplifying a method he used repeatedly in the 1930s, Matisse amplified an existing theme in *Music* (1939, left) by adding a second figure to the previous month's painting of Hélène Galitzine alone playing the guitar.

L eft: a 1941
photograph of
Matisse perched on a
stool as he worked on
Nymph in the Forest.
The shafts of the trees
resemble beams of anti-
aircraft searchlights; the
world was at war.

O verleaf left: darkness
replaced light
in *Reader on a Black
Background,* painted
in Paris in August 1939.

O verleaf right:
in *Woman in
Blue/The Large Blue Robe
and Mimosas* (1937),
Lydia Delectorskaya
is shown wearing the
ruffled dress featured
in many of the drawings
and paintings Matisse
did that year.

exist because of changing
customs,' he said in
1952. 'There will be
mural painting.' But
no mural commissions
materialized.

Drawings, engravings and illustrations

Instead, Matisse
concentrated on designs
for tapestries, including two versions of *Window at
Tahiti* (1935) and *Nymph in the Forest* (1936–43). The only
design actually to be woven, *Window at Tahiti (I)*, did
not turn out as well as the artist had hoped. A 1938
commission to decorate an overmantel in Nelson A.
Rockefeller's New York apartment resulted in a work
more loosely structured than easel paintings from the
same period, such as *Large Reclining Nude/The Pink
Nude* (1935), *Woman in Blue* (1937) and *Music* (1939).

Even more than the decorative paintings he repeatedly
made until the late 1930s, drawing allowed Matisse to
fully investigate the female figure. The many nudes from
this period include rough sketches, paintings with drawing
subsequently added, engravings and book illustrations.

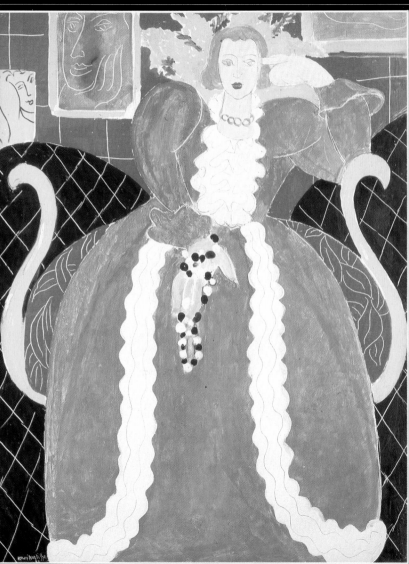

He wrote in 1947, 'I want to bring my painting in line with my drawings – the ones that come straight from the heart, done with the utmost simplicity – so I have started down a very arduous road that seems inordinately long because of the little time remaining to me at my age.'

'A character called Pain' (Louis Aragon)

Matisse was taken ill and had to go to hospital in September 1937; his convalescence would be long. He and his wife legally separated. 'A character called Pain,' to quote Louis Aragon, had made its entrance. The character would bide its time and reappear later on.

In late 1938 Matisse moved out of his Place Charles-Félix apartment and into the Régina, a huge hotel in Cimiez, up in the hills above Nice, that had been built in

M atisse shared his thoughts about *The Dream* (left) with a friend. 'I found a lovely old Romanian blouse,' he wrote, 'a blouse with faded red *petit point* embroidery that must have belonged to a princess, and if only I could find lots more, I'd trade a beautiful drawing for them. It's taken me a year to do this painting – people who see nothing but the way I've depicted her hair and the embroidery on her shoulder think I'm not being serious – but you know better.'

O pposite above: Matisse drawing the model Wilma Javor in his Paris studio in the summer of 1939. A drawing of the same model appears in *Reader on a Black Background.* Behind Matisse is a self-portrait the artist sketched with his eyes closed.

O pposite below: in November 1938 Matisse moved into the gigantic Hôtel Régina.

1897 for winter visitors from England, including Queen Victoria. A phase in his career had drawn to a close. His Nice period ended with *The Dream* (1940), a painting of a dozing model in a Romanian blouse.

In this period he designed the scenery and costumes for a Ballets Russes production of the symphonic ballet *Red and Black*, with music by Dmitri Shostakovich and choreography by Léonide Massine. The backdrop behind the dancers featured the same slanting swathes of colour that march across the Barnes Foundation *Dance* mural.

Matisse went to Geneva in August 1939, intending to take in an exhibition of masterpieces from the Prado, but he never managed to see it. War was imminent, and he was forced to leave the city at once. Upon his return to Paris he designed a cover for the magazine *Verve*: bits of stained-glass colour sprinkled across an overwhelming field of black, the same 'Manet black' that appeared in the pictures he had painted that summer in Paris. He went to the cinema and raved about Jean Renoir's film *The Rules of the Game*. He spent time in southwestern France with his

'It's been my favourite painting for a number of years,' Matisse said of the 1941 *Still Life with a Magnolia* (left). His handwritten instructions to the photoengraver of the magazine *Verve* spelled out exactly how he wanted it printed, colour by colour, object by object. The central pot, for example: 'Venetian red, black border; (handle, left) Venetian red, black border; (handle, right) yellow ochre and white; (bottom) the bottom of the kettle a single layer of moderate cadmium yellow over scarlet lake scumble.'

assistant and model Lydia Delectorskaya and did some drawing and painting there.

Matisse's friends and his son Pierre urged him to leave the country. At one point he considered sailing to Algeria or Martinique but decided against it and spent the time painting in Nice. In May 1940, when German troops invaded France, he was in Paris, making arrangements for a trip to Brazil. He immediately cancelled his plans, explaining in a letter to Pierre that if he had left he'd 'have felt like a deserter'. He headed back to Nice and, despite (or because of) the 'general anxiety' and 'constant uneasiness' so 'detrimental to the workings of the unconscious', picked up where he had left off. But there was something else spurring him to work 'unceasingly, with a feeling that time was precious' – he had been diagnosed as having cancer.

Wartime

On 17 January 1941 Matisse underwent surgery for duodenal cancer in Lyons. 'Give me the three or four years I need to finish my work,' he told his doctors. While convalescing he worked on a series of drawings that were later collected and published as *Themes and Variations*, with a preface by Louis Aragon. A young night nurse, Monique Bourgeois (a 'splendid individual'), became his model for a series of paintings.

In June 1943 Matisse left Nice, by then a potential

Allied bombing target, and moved to the villa Le Rêve in the hill town of Vence, which reminded him of Tahiti. In Vence he turned out a series of interiors that proved to be the summation and distillation of 'a lifetime of labour' – and the grand finale of his career as a painter.

At the same time, paper cutouts began to spread across the walls of his room. After using them to help him compose the Barnes *Dance* mural, Matisse found them well suited to his preparatory work for *Large Reclining Nude/The Pink Nude*; he also used cutouts when designing the covers of the third and fourth issues of the magazine *Cahiers d'Art*. From this melding of line, colour and sculptural space would evolve a number of decorative silkscreens and the book *Jazz*, which Matisse worked on throughout the war.

In 1944 Matisse learned that his ex-wife and daughter, who were active in the Resistance, had been arrested by the Gestapo. Amélie Matisse was sentenced to six months in prison. He heard no word from Marguerite for months;

Monique Bourgeois went on duty as Matisse's nurse on 26 September 1942 and soon started to sit for many drawings and paintings, including *Idol* (above) from December 1942. Matisse was to continue his 'flirtation of sorts' with her even after she became Sister Jacques-Marie. 'I'm tempted to spell that *flowertation*,' he wrote, 'because it's a little as though we tossed flowers at each other's faces'. Their affectionate give-and-take lasted right through the building of the Chapel of the Rosary at Vence.

she was tortured but managed to escape before being sent to the camps. Still, he continued to produce drawings and book illustrations. After the Liberation of Paris, on 25 August 1944, the artist was able to resume trips to the capital, where his work was exhibited and honoured. On 26 July 1945 the magazine *Arts* celebrated the artist's first trip to Paris since 1940 with an article called 'Matisse Is Back'.

He was honoured with a major exhibition at the Salon d'Automne. He and Picasso had simultaneous one-artist shows at the Victoria and Albert Museum in London. An issue of *Verve* was devoted to him, and his work went on view at the Galerie Maeght in Paris. The Musée National d'Art Moderne purchased several of his paintings. Missing were the decorative paintings that had vanished during the war, were on exhibit abroad or were hidden from public view. Back in Vence in 1946 and 1947, he spent his time painting the large interiors featured in a special issue of *Verve* (1948).

The Chapel of the Rosary at Vence

At the end of 1947 he was finally given the opportunity to create on French soil, in the very place he himself had

A 'page of writing' intended for private contemplation, the design for *The Stations of the Cross* (top and above, in the unfinished Chapel of the Rosary in Vence) was executed in two hours, 'in a single burst of inspiration'.

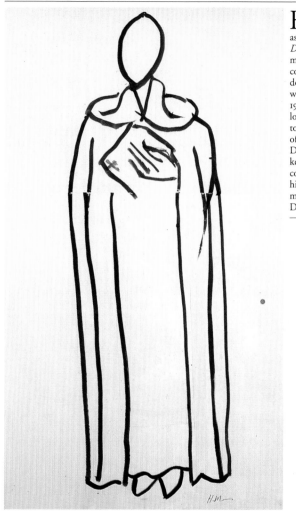

Faceless icon of lofty ideals and spiritual asceticism, the *Saint Dominic* ceramic-tile mural was preceded by countless studies, some done full scale on studio walls; this one dates from 1949 to 1950. Matisse long pondered how best to represent the 'athlete of Christ' of the Dominican tradition. He kept trying different configurations until he hit upon the one that most fully conveyed the Dominican message.

chosen for the quality of its light, an 'architectural painting' that would prove to be the culmination of his 'previous investigations'.

On the recommendation of Matisse's former nurse, now Sister Jacques-Marie, Brother Rayssiguier, a Dominican novice eager to revive religious art, talked to

Matisse about a chapel being planned near his villa. A few minutes into their initial discussion, and the chapel was 'done'. Matisse immediately saw the project as a chance to apply his paper-cutout technique to stained-glass windows. As in *Jazz*, the chapel would balance the windows against facing 'pages of writing': the ceramic-tile murals *The Stations of the Cross*, *Virgin and Child* and *Saint Dominic*.

Matisse channelled all of his time and energy into this project until 1951. The Chapel of the Rosary was to be the last of his 'symphonic interiors', his masterpiece

Late in life, Matisse produced a great many drawings of masklike faces (*Mask*, 1950, below left) on large sheets of painted white paper and inserted them among the organic motifs of the paper cutouts he pinned to his studio walls.

– a white studio in which all colours could come together. Early in 1949 Matisse left Vence and moved back to the Hôtel Régina, which could more easily accommodate full-scale maquettes for the chapel. He pinned his paper-cutout studies for stained-glass windows and chasubles up on walls that over the next four years were to serve as composition boards for large-scale independent cutouts. The 'garden behind a colonnade' he had envisioned for the chapel began to overrun the interior of his studio. The chapel was constructed slowly and was consecrated on 25 June 1951. Matisse's health made it impossible for him to attend.

The charcoal lines visible in *Blue Nude (IV)* (1952, above right), last in a series of paper-cutout nudes done between September 1951 and June 1952, show that it evolved through numerous preparatory sessions.

From 1950 on Matisse made many independent paper cutouts, many in a shape based on the Vence chapel windows. In 1954, after a stay in the country, a debilitated Matisse returned to Nice at the end of the summer. 'On 15 October,' Marguerite later recalled, 'he had begun the rose window for Mrs Nelson Rockefeller's

The philosopher Henri Bergson said that the never-ending process of growth and creation propels life to ever-higher levels. A depiction of *élan vital*, the life force, *The*

chapel [Union Church, Pocantico Hills, New York], and he kept reworking the design until the moment he died,' on 3 November 1954.

Using a piece of charcoal attached to the end of a very long bamboo pole, he had outlined the huge smiling faces of his grandchildren on the ceiling over his bed. In a corner of his room, near the last of his paper cutouts (*The Vine* and *The Wild Poppies*), his first window design for the Vence chapel, the enigmatic horseman of *Celestial Jerusalem* – symbol of Matisse's entire life – carried on the struggle, armed with the pure forces of red, blue, yellow and green.

Sheaf (1953, left), surges with energy.

Overleaf: *The Clown*, from *Jazz* (1947, left), and Matisse in Vence (1948, right).

DOCUMENTS

Matisse the painter, as revealed
through his own incisive statements,
and Matisse the man, as seen through
the eyes of his contemporaries.

Matisse on Matisse

Matisse seldom disclosed much about himself. In his frequent letters to family and friends, he shared his thoughts about his evolving oeuvre. He was self critical and obsessive about clarity. In personal matters, however, he rarely strayed from the bare essentials, as if discussing himself were an obligation to be only grudgingly fulfilled.

A short autobiography

When a French magazine asked Matisse for some words about himself for its first issue, he set aside the personal and submitted the following curriculum vitae, devoted almost exclusively to his career as a painter.

Born 31 December 1869 at Le Cateau-Cambrésis. 1887: admitted to law school. 1892: admitted to Gustave Moreau's studio, Ecole des Beaux-Arts. Worked at the Musée du Louvre after Poussin, Raphael, Chardin, David de Heem, Philippe de Champaigne, etc. 1894: first public exhibition, Société Nationale des Beaux-Arts, Champ-de-Mars. Working vacations in Brittany and Mediterranean coast. 1904: Druet exhibition. Public opinion at the time against the 'Fauves'. Gradual acceptance of our outlook. Numerous exhibitions of paintings, sculpture, engravings. Uninterrupted work ever since, with trips to Spain, Italy, Germany, Russia, Algeria and England.

At first my painting conformed with the dark register of the masters I studied at the Louvre. Then my palette brightened. Influence of Impressionists, Neo-Impressionists, Cézanne and Oriental art. Spots of colour combined with arabesques became the building blocks of my pictures (for this period: Municipal Museum, Moscow; collections Tescenlind, Copenhagen and Marcel Sembat, Paris).

Around 1914, this eminently decorative style began to shift towards a planar approach in greater depth, towards the intimacy of my current work.

Henri Matisse.

Exceedingly regular work schedule, day in, day out, morning to evening.

A few books and articles have been written about my work. They may provide you with information about the relation between my painting and contemporary trends. These include: *Henri Matisse* (Nouvelle Revue Française); *Henri Matisse* (Crès), and Fels' *Henri Matisse* (Chroniques du Jour).

Formes, January 1930

Of meals and music

Matisse described his daily regimen, which revolved completely around his work, to a friend in Nice.

A little later, I asked Matisse over to dinner. He replied that he never ate in the evening but would be glad to drop by after dinner. When he did I was quite naturally curious to know why he did not dine.

'Over the last ten or twelve years,' he explained, 'I've noticed that the midday meal tides me over. Eating's a real pleasure when you're hungry.... I like to eat around noon – and I eat like a horse – after which I take a little nap to digest my food. But if I eat again come evening, I feel sluggish and get nightmares that wake me up. I retire at ten o'clock, and I get up around six in the morning, partly because I want to take advantage of as much light as I possibly can. I enjoy nearly perfect health.... Better than when I was twenty. Everyone has to find his own pace of living. I drink very little, usually dilute my wine or take a glass of beer; no hard liquor, no overindulgence of any kind....'

Several times he alluded to music to illustrate specific points he would make about painting. I finally came

around to asking him if he liked music.

'Yes, very much so. It's my sole form of relaxation. I play the violin, have ever since I was a child. But the more accomplished I became as an artist, the less satisfied I was with playing the violin so poorly.

'A music teacher told me that if I practised for a year, I would achieve the level of relative proficiency I desired, so I took lessons for a year and often spent six hours a day playing. The result is that now I (and on occasion my friends) can get some enjoyment out of my playing.'

Frank Harris
Macula, 1976

Twenty questions

Simple answers to simple questions.

1. Q: How would you explain your paintings to a child?
   A: Either this pleases you or this does not please.
2. Q: What is your feeling about abstract painting?
   A: It is a problem which is relative to each person.
3. Q: What was the greatest single influence on your art – Giotto, Fra Angelico? Byzantine mosaics? Persian miniatures?
   A: All these and, above all, Cézanne.
4. Q: Do you get more creative pleasure out of working on secular or religious subjects?
   A: I bring all subjects back to human sentiments.
5. Q: Which painter has exerted the most influence on you?
   A: Cézanne.
6. Q: What clues can you give for better appreciating your work?

A: No answer.

7. Q: What influence do you consider your sculpture has had on your paintings?

A: A familiarity with solid forms, to supplement the study of nature through drawing.

8. Q: Which do you consider more important in your own work and in art generally – line or colour?

A: Both.

9. Q: What do you think is your most creative contribution in the use of colour?

A: I have brought a feeling of space through colour.

10. Q: Which of your paintings do you consider is completely realized in this respect?

A: No answer.

11. Q: Why have you given up your absorption with colour, mass and form and seemingly gone in the direction of line?

A: An error. I am always taken by colour.

12. Q: Which do you consider more important – your paper cutouts or your paintings?

A: Both.

13. Q: Why did you give your paintings to the museum in Le Cateau?

A: Because it is my native village.

14. Q: Do any of the younger living artists arouse your enthusiasm?

A: No answer.

15. Q: What advice would you give to young painters?

A: To draw a great deal and not to reflect too much.

16. Q: Should an art student begin to work with line first, or with colour, or with both at once?

A: That depends on his temperament; in principle, both

of them, and harmonizing them will be his big difficulty.

17. Q: Do you consider the allied arts such as music, literature, etc., important to the development of a painter?

A: Very important.

18. Q: What do you consider the most creative period in your life?

A: Each period has had its importance, but I should be tempted to say this one.

19. Q: What direction do you think modern art will take?

A: Light.

20. Q: Do you consider that in your collages you have found the final solution to your art?

A: No. I have not finished.

'Matisse Answers Twenty Questions'
Look magazine, 25 August 1953

Learning in a cabaret

After spending his formative years copying in the galleries of the Louvre, Matisse kept on working outside his studio in search of a personal interpretation of the world that would transcend mere transcription.

Each day I need to recover my idea of the previous day. Even in the early days I was like that and I envied my comrades who could work anywhere. At Montmartre, Debray, the proprietor of the Moulin de la Galette, used to invite all the painters to come and scribble at his place. [Kees] van Dongen was prodigious. He ran around after the dancers and drew them at the same time. Naturally I took advantage of the invitation too, but all I managed to do was learn the tune of the farandole, which everyone used to roar out as

soon as the orchestra played it:
      'Let's pray to God for those who're nearly broke!
      'Let's pray to God for those who've not a bean!'
Do you remember it? And later, this tune helped me when I began my painting of *La Danse* which is in the Barnes Collection.... I whistled it as I painted. I almost danced.... Those were good times.

from Francis Carco
'Conversation with Matisse', 1941
trans. in Jack Flam, *Matisse on Art*, 1973

On influence

Matisse surrounded himself with other artists and their work – which, he believed, was one way for him to develop and grow.

I have never avoided the influence of others. I would have considered this a cowardice and lack of sincerity toward myself. I believe that the personality of the artist develops and asserts itself through the struggles it has to go through when pitted against other personalities. If the fight is fatal and the personality succumbs, it means that this was bound to be its fate.

from Guillaume Apollinaire
Interview with Henri Matisse, 1907
trans. in Jack Flam, *Matisse on Art*, 1973

Tahiti

Although constantly on the move, Matisse did relatively little long-distance travelling. After his 1930 trip to the South

Matisse at work on a sketch for the *Saint Dominic* mural in the chapel at Vence (1949). A sketch for *The Stations of the Cross* mural is hanging on the right.

Pacific, he returned time and again, through memory, in his studio.

Did your stay in Tahiti have a great influence on your work?

The stay in Tahiti was very profitable. I very much wanted to experience light on the other side of the Equator, to have contact with its trees and to penetrate what is there. Each light offers its own harmony. It's a different atmosphere. The light of the Pacific, of the islands, is a deep golden goblet into which you look.

I remember that first of all, on my arrival, it was disappointing. And then, little by little, it was beautiful…it is beautiful! The leaves of the high coconut palms, blown back by the trade winds, made a silky sound. The sound of the leaves could be heard along with the orchestral roar of the sea waves, waves which broke over the reefs surrounding the island.

I used to bathe in the lagoon. I swam around brilliant corals emphasized by the sharp black accents of holothurians. I would plunge my head into the water, transparent above the absinthe bottom of the lagoon, my eyes wide open…and then suddenly I would lift my head above the water and gaze at the luminous whole. The contrasts…

Tahiti…the Islands…But the tranquil desert island doesn't exist. Our European worries accompany us there. Indeed there were no cares on this island. The Europeans were bored. They were comfortably waiting to retire in a stuffy torpor, and doing nothing to interest themselves or to defeat their boredom; they did not even think anymore. Above them and all around them, there was this wonderful light of the first day, all this splendour; but they didn't see how good it was any more.

They had closed the factories and the natives wallowed in animal pleasures. A beautiful country, asleep in the bright heat of the sun.

No, the tranquil desert island, the solitary paradise doesn't exist. One would be quickly bored there because one would have no problems.

from André Verdet
Interview with Henri Matisse, 1952
trans. in Jack Flam, *Matisse on Art*, 1973

'To paint carefree and undisturbed'

While designing the Vence chapel, Matisse identified so closely with his project that at one point he expressed a wish to become a monk – only his religion was painting.

I should like to live like a monk in his cell, so long as I have what I need to paint carefree and undisturbed. All my life I have been influenced by the opinion current at the time I first began to paint, when it was permissible only to render observations made from nature, when all that derived from the imagination or memory was called bogus and worthless for the construction of a plastic work. The teachers at the [Ecole des] Beaux-Arts used to say to their pupils, 'Copy nature stupidly'.

Throughout my career I have reacted against this attitude to which I could not submit; and this struggle has been the source of the different stages along my route, in the course of which I have searched for means of expression beyond the literal copy – such as Divisionism and Fauvism.

These rebellions led me to study each element of construction: drawing, colour, values, composition; to explore how these elements could be combined

A photograph Matisse took in Tahiti (1930).

into a synthesis without diminishing the eloquence of any one of them by the presence of the others, and to make constructions from these elements with their intrinsic qualities undiminished in combination; in other words, to respect the purity of the means.

Each generation of artists views the production of the previous generation differently. The paintings of the Impressionists, constructed with pure colours, made the next generation see that these colours, if they can be used to describe objects or natural phenomena, contain within them, independently of the objects that they serve to express, the power to affect the feelings of those who look at them.

Thus simple colours can act upon the inner feelings with more force, the simpler they are. A blue, for example, accompanied by the brilliance of its complementaries, acts upon the feelings like a sharp blow on a gong. The same

with red and yellow; and the artist must be able to sound them when he needs to.

In the Chapel my chief aim was to balance a surface of light and colour against a solid wall with black drawing on a white background.

This Chapel is for me the culmination of a life of work, and the coming into flower of an enormous, sincere and difficult effort. This is not a work that I chose, but rather a work for which I was chosen by fate, towards the end of a course that I am still continuing according to my researches; the Chapel has afforded me the possibility of realizing them by uniting them.

I foresee that this work will not be in vain and that it may remain the expression of a period in art, perhaps now left behind, though I do not believe so. It is impossible to be sure about this today, before the new movements have been fully realized.

Whatever weaknesses this expression

of human feeling may contain will fall away of their own accord, but there will remain a living part which will unite the past with the future of the plastic tradition.

I hope that this part, which I call my revelation, is expressed with sufficient power to be fertilizing and to return to its source.

'La Chapelle du Rosaire'
in *Chapelle du Rosaire des Dominicaines de Vence*, 1951
trans. in Jack Flam, *Matisse on Art*, 1973

'The olive trees are so beautiful'

Matisse's friendship with Charles Camoin began when they were both students in Gustave Moreau's studio at the Ecole des Beaux-Arts.

I've been working in the sun all this time, from 10 to noon, and I'm exhausted for the rest of the day. I'm going to change my schedule – as of tomorrow I start at 6:30 or 7 in the morning. That should give me a good hour or two of work. The olive trees are so beautiful then – high noon is superb, but oppressive. I think Cézanne captured its tonal harmonies very well, but not, fortunately, its glare, which is unbearable. A little while ago I took a nap under an olive tree, and the color harmonies I saw there were so touching. It's like a paradise you have no right to analyze, but you are a painter, for God's sake! Nice is so beautiful! A light so soft and tender, despite its brilliance. I don't know why it often reminds me of the Touraine (should that have two *r*'s?). The Touraine light is a little more golden; here is it silvery. Even though the objects it touches have rich colors – the greens, for example, I often break

my back trying to paint them. Having written that, I let my eyes wander the room where some of my old daubings are hanging, and it occurs to me that I may have hit the mark once in a while after all, though I can't be sure.

Henri Matisse to Charles Camoin
23 May 1918
trans. in Jack Flam, *Matisse: A Retrospective*, 1988

On style

In another letter to Camoin, Matisse proposed a redefinition of so-called decorative 'grand style'.

Don't you think that this is a slightly one-sided view of the matter, and that you can do outlines in a mere semblance of the grand style or half-tones in a genuine grand style? Who had the greater style, Gauguin or Corot? I believe that style comes from the order and nobility of the artist's mind, whether the order is acquired and developed or entirely intuitive, which is perhaps the consequence of order. But if it results from a particular slant, it yields no more than half-tones. This is said without pretensions...

Henri Matisse to Charles Camoin
2 May 1918
trans. in Jack Flam, *Matisse: A Retrospective*, 1988

An English model

The dream of the poet and writer André Rouveyre becomes Matisse's reality.

You mention an English girl you dreamed about. An hour ago I had a third drawing session with an English girl more beautiful, perhaps, than the one that you told me about who eventually faded away. Mine is still here and will come back the day after tomorrow to look me in the eyes the way people usually do when I am working, that is, defencelessly, with nothing to worry or protect them. Her lovely, changeable eyes looked hazel to me yesterday, but today I couldn't make out their colour. I asked Lydia to come and tell me what colour they really were. The colour of her eyes, she replied, was the same as mine, of hers. That quite astonished me. But as the sitting progressed I noticed that her eyes changed, grew darker as her face became flushed – not because of anything I had done, I swear – and it occurred to me that it was the rush of blood that was causing her eyes to change colour. You can't imagine the delectable harmony of her eyes, lips, and gently curving chin. I'll never find a way of conveying that. She sits before me like a frightened little pigeon in my hand. [My] English girl certainly measures up to yours. Only mine will be coming back for at least the next fortnight.

> Henri Matisse to André Rouveyre
> 5 April 1947

Awaiting the thunderbolt

How do you paint a still life? The first step is to surround yourself with the 'prettiest girls'.

I am trying hard to settle down to my work. Before arriving here I had intended to paint flowers and fruits – I have set up several arrangements in my studio – but the kind of uncertainty in which we are living here makes it impossible; consequently I am afraid to start working face-to-face with objects which

Matisse in his Vence garden (c. 1943–4).

I have to animate myself with my own feelings— Therefore I have arranged with some motion picture agents to send me their prettiest girls – if I don't keep them I give them ten francs. And thus I have three or four young and pretty models whom I have pose separately for drawing, three hours in the morning, three hours in the afternoon. This keeps me in the midst of my flowers and fruits with which I can get in touch gradually without being aware of it. Sometimes I stop in front of a motif, a corner of my studio which I find expressive, yet quite beyond myself and my strength, and I await the thunderbolt which cannot fail to come. This saps all my vitality.

> Henri Matisse to Pierre Matisse
> 1 September 1940
> trans. in Jack Flam, *Matisse: A Retrospective*, 1988

Henri Matisse at home

In both Issy-les-Moulineaux and Nice, Monday was Matisse's day to catch up on correspondence, attend to business and talk painting with writers, painters, biographers and close friends.

Picasso and Françoise Gilot at home in La Galloise, Vallauris (1951).

Matisse and Picasso

Matisse's relationship with Pablo Picasso was nothing short of electric. Françoise Gilot, Picasso's companion from 1943 to 1953, reported on the give-and-take between the two artists in her memoirs – and gave the advantage to Matisse.

[Matisse] had a kind of paternal attitude toward Pablo and that… helped, because in friendship it was always Pablo who took and the others who gave. In their meetings, the active side was Pablo; the passive, Matisse. Pablo always sought to charm Matisse, like a dancer, but in the end it was Matisse who conquered Pablo.

'We must talk to each other as much as we can,' he told Pablo one day. 'When one of us dies, there will be some things the other will never be able to talk of with anyone else.'

Later, when Matisse was again living in his apartment at the Hôtel Régina in Cimiez, we used to go see him about every two weeks. Very often Pablo would bring him his latest paintings or drawings, and sometimes I would bring canvases and drawings of mine. Matisse would have Lydia show us things he had just done, or if he had been working on *papiers découpés*, we would see them pinned up on the walls.

One day when we called, Matisse had just bought a Chinese mandarin's mauve-pink silk robe, very long and lined with the fur of a Gobi desert tiger. It stood up all by itself, and Matisse had posed it in front of a pale mauve Arab wall hanging. The robe was very thick, with a high white collar that flared up on each side of the face.

'I'm going to have my new model pose in it,' Matisse said, 'but first I'd like to see what it looks like on Françoise.' Pablo didn't like the idea but Matisse insisted, so I tried on the Chinese robe. It came right up to the top of my head and I was completely engulfed in its triangular form. Matisse said, 'Oh, I could do something very good with that.'

'If you do,' Pablo said, 'you'll have to give me the painting and give her the coat.'

Matisse began to back down. 'Well,' he said, 'the robe looks nice on Françoise, but it wouldn't be at all right for your painting.'

'I don't mind,' Pablo said.

'No,' Matisse said, 'I've got something that's much better suited to you. It's from New Guinea. It's a full-sized human figure that's completely savage. It's just right for you.' Lydia went out to get it. It was carved in arborescent fern, streaked with violent

tones of blue, yellow, and red, very barbaric looking and not really old. It was larger than life-size, rather battered, its legs attached by strings – just bits and pieces barely hanging together, topped by a feathered head. It was much less handsome than many things of New Guinea I had seen. Pablo looked at it and said that we didn't have room in the car to carry it away. He promised Matisse he'd send for it another day.

Matisse acquiesced. 'But before you go, I want you to see my plane tree,' he said. I wondered how he had managed to bring a plane tree into his hotel apartment. At that point a giant of a girl, who looked about twenty years old and was surely six feet tall, walked in.

'This is my plane tree,' Matisse said, beaming.

After we had left, Pablo said, 'Did you notice how Lydia's nose was out of joint? Something's going on there, you may be sure. But don't you find that a little exaggerated, for him to be carrying on like that with women, at his age? He ought to be a little more serious than that…. Besides, that New Guinea thing frightens me. I think it probably frightens Matisse too and that's why he's so eager to get rid of it. He thinks I'll be able to exorcise it better than he can.'

Shortly after that visit, Pablo went back to Paris and stayed there a while, but all during the time he was away Matisse held fast to his idea. He called up the Ramiés at the pottery, not knowing that Pablo had left for Paris, and said that the object was still there waiting for him. Then he wrote to him twice reminding him that his gift was still uncalled for. He obviously had his heart set on transferring it to Pablo's possession. 'It's not something you can

P ortrait of Louis Aragon by Matisse (1942).

remain indifferent to,' he wrote. 'And it's not sad, either.' But Pablo was still put out to think that Matisse believed it was better adapted to his temperament than something Chinese. He didn't like the idea of Matisse thinking that *he* was the intelligent painter and Pablo just a creature of instinct. Finally, Matisse had it sent over to Vallauris. Once Pablo had it, he was rather happy about it and we made a special trip to Cimiez just so he could thank Matisse.

Françoise Gilot and Carlton Lake
Life with Picasso, 1965

Louis Aragon comes calling

The wonderfully digressive portrait of Matisse that the French Surrealist writer Aragon paints offers a rare glimpse of the emotional underpinnings of the painter's creativity.

So at long last I had gone to see the painter in his palace. Somehow or other the thought had occurred to me that I might write a book about Matisse which would indirectly be a portrait of him. I had begun. I went almost daily to see my subject. I made him alter his pose, he consented. The lighting varied. Time passed. There was a sudden noisy white flutter of wings from the birds in the great aviary. I prowled round my model; I had to understand the shoulder, the way the branches grew out of the trunk… And then suddenly he began talking about his journey to Morocco, about a woman he had seen from a taxi, about a piece of stuff. The difference between painters and myself is that they work towards a likeness by means of sketches and rough drafts, while in my case what I write winds about the subject like an endless tangled ribbon, I cut nothing, I throw away nothing, and finally the portrait is the sum of my thoughts, about my model and about countless other things when I raise my eyes to look out of the window or at the telephone… In short, what painters call a portrait is not what I call a portrait when I am writing.

Especially on certain days, in spite of the bright sunshine, or even when dusk fell, a sudden star-shaped pucker would appear on Matisse's cheek and his lips would grow pale. He said nothing, and I pretended to have seen nothing. On one such occasion, noticing my hesitant speech, he asked me: 'What's the matter with you?' With me? Nothing. Once serenity was restored, I had the sense of having myself experienced that furtive stab of pain. I looked into the shadows, behind Henri Matisse, imagining I had seen a blurred figure there, sneering. The fancies one has…

Matisse runs his hand over the juxtaposed drawings that cover the walls of his Nice studio (c. 1940–1).

H enri Matisse, photographed by Henri Cartier-Bresson in 1944.

Caelumque…
In the room we are in now, in Matisse's room at Cimiez, there is a sky, a strange potential sky, which is not on the ceiling but on the walls surrounding those women's faces which the God of this place has rendered sublime, often in the etymological sense of *uplifted*. It is a white sky, Matisse's sky. Against that sky the faces or the still lifes have been inscribed without blurring it, carefully preserving the uniform whiteness of the air. The line, the way it unfolds, the way it limits surfaces have all been calculated so as to respect that whiteness. Matisse is fully conscious of the whiteness thus maintained. He has repeatedly pointed it out to me, as also, in his book illustrations, his respect for the lay-out of the page, the balance kept

between text and drawing… One can't help remembering a line of Mallarmé's: *Le blanc souci* ['*Le blanc souci de notre toile*', 'Salut']… True, but the poet's cult of the empty page, that reverent dread of blackening it, is something the painter feels only to begin with, for he has – and he knows he has – the gift of not blackening the page, and I would readily assert that the sheet of paper on which he has traced a line is whiter than the virgin sheet it was. Whiter, because it is conscious of its whiteness.

With a sweeping gesture of his hand, Matisse shows the walls covered with sets of drawings in close juxtaposition: 'You see,' he says, 'it's the same whiteness everywhere… I haven't removed it anywhere…'

White everywhere. A strange game of dominoes. Between my visits these dominoes, changing their position with the majestic slowness of chessmen, finish their game with a few more moves, and other drawings are added to the incomplete set, wherever there's room, as it were blank/four, blank/…

Louis Aragon
Henri Matisse: A Novel
trans. Jean Stewart, 1972

Life with 'the Boss'

From her unique vantage point as an eyewitness to life in the Hôtel Régina, Jacqueline Duhême chronicled the flow of Matisse's daily routine and his seasonal migration between Paris and Nice, and paused to mention the special light in the artist's residences.

He was sitting in an armchair, dressed in beige fine wool trousers and a loose-fitting jacket of matching material with a small pointed collar. Long afterwards I learned that Matisse had his apparel made to order at Charvet's on Place Vendôme, just as his friend Pierre Reverdy did. Under his unbuttoned jacket he wore a granny-smith green jersey and a pink shirt. His face was framed by a short white beard that had been neatly trimmed. His alert, piercing blue eyes, youthful for a man of seventy-nine, looked out from behind small gold-rimmed spectacles.

In this bright, spacious room were the master's white bed, drawings on the walls, plants and, in a wooden cage, the turtledoves we had heard earlier. Pink earthenware on the furniture. The only dab of blue in this space: Matisse's eyes, changing from pale to navy blue.

At his request, I went and bought a few sheets of ordinary beige wrapping paper and some sheets of light and blue paper, the kind used to cover schoolbooks. He then pinned these sheets to the wall, first alongside, then underneath each other, alternating shades. Then using white Ingres paper Matisse cut out his subjects, gulls or fish, the forms of which he had decided upon in the course of his preparatory work. His sureness of hand never failed to amaze me. He then stepped back and asked me to affix the cutouts to the coloured backdrop. This operation was carried out with the help of pointers. I rearranged the various elements of the composition as he indicated....

Matisse's day went like clockwork. It began at 8 AM: The entire 'staff – Lydia, myself, the cook and the housekeeper – had to be ready. Everyone at his post. The night nurse had seen to the 'morning treatment of the Boss and washed and dressed him. Off she'd go to sleep. The cook had his *café au lait* and bread and jam already prepared, and had taken out his medicine. I would bring it all in

Christmas postcard from Matisse to Jacqueline Duhême in 1948.

à aragon
Henri matisse
nov. 46

E lsa with a Veil, one in a series of drawings
Matisse did of Louis Aragon's wife in 1946.

on a tray. Freshly shaven and smelling of eau-de-cologne, Monsieur Matisse would be sitting in bed, propped up by some cushions. The impeccably fitted sheets were dotted with embroidered daisies. As he loved to smoke cigarillos, the lighted tip would often drop on to the back of the sheet and burn a hole in it.

Whereupon he would insist on its being mended, not as a cheerless repair, but transformed into an embroidered daisy.

He shared breakfast with the cats on his bed. He'd listen to the news on the radio, then wash his hands and settle down to work. Since his operation he

had been confined to bed for all but one or two hours a day, so he really needed someone to assist him. He would work until lunchtime. Just then he was doing preliminary drawings for the illustrated *Letters of a Portuguese Nun.* Since he needed a face, he used me as a model. Because he didn't like motionless poses, he would have me sharpen pencils or coat pieces of paper with gouache. He used lots of painted paper, but he insisted on its being prepared at home. That was how I learned to brush superb cobalt blue and other colours on to paper….

The Boss could spend as long as an entire week labouring over a charcoal portrait. Then he would start all over. He seemed to be committing its contours, volumes and lighting to memory so that he could then produce a pure drawing with a single brushstroke…. It was thrilling. You could sense his restraint; his concentration filled the room.

After working all morning, lunch, then a nap.

In the afternoon Matisse would get out of bed. He'd walk inside the house, sometimes go for a stroll in town, call on friends….

The Boss also enjoyed being surrounded by objects he had selected and positioned in a very precise manner. They had to be located where he could see them. After wiping a pot on a piece of furniture, one had to be careful to put it back exactly the way one found it, with the handle turned to the right, for example. Nothing around Matisse was arranged haphazardly. He kept an eagle eye on the forms around him and remembered them.

He was thrifty and occasionally got up and rummaged through the house to see if anything that might still be usable had been thrown away. This scavenging took me aback. He explained to me that his parents were not wealthy when he was small. His brother and he had to moisten their fingers with saliva and pick up seeds that had fallen between the floor tiles. Once they had gleaned a hundred grams of seed, their father would reward them with a sou....

Around 5 PM Matisse would take a cup of weak tea, and we'd work some more until dinner. After the meal, he enjoyed having me read to him a while. At one time it was Chateaubriand's *Mémoires d'outre-tombe*....

In late June we would leave for Paris, where Henri Matisse kept an apartment on the Boulevard Montparnasse. That was his home for the entire summer. He felt it was too hot in the south of France, and too crowded.

The SNCF [the French National Railways] provided us with a special car complete with a 'parlour and large couchette' for the Boss. Lydia occupied the couchette adjoining the 'suite', while the nurse, the cook and I were assigned the next three couchettes. The cats had been committed to the gardener's care back in Vence. Our arrival at the Gare de Lyon attracted considerable attention, and I took not a little pride in numbering among the 'Henri Matisse contingent'. Once we were ensconced in Paris – a respectable third-floor apartment in an affluent ashlar-masonry building – we fell back into our customary tempo of living.

Many visitors came calling. Edmonde Charles-Roux, a young journalist, for an interview. Roland Petit, in need of sets for his ballets, which Matisse was unwilling to do. Louis Aragon,

requesting a portrait of his wife as an illustration for *Elsa's Eyes*....

One afternoon, Yvette Chauviré, featured soloist with the Paris Opéra ballet, showed up to perform *The Dying Swan*, 'Lifarian' style, for Henri Matisse. It was amazing to watch a dancer's every movement at such close range. We could see the tremendous exertion, the iron discipline that underlies the delicacy of dancing, its seeming effortlessness. Pencil in mid-air, Matisse would gaze intently at her movements as if hypnotized by their beauty.

Summer was drawing to a close, so we got ready to head back to Nice. This time we would be staying at the Régina. The apartment entrance consisted of a splendid hall of palatial proportions. When you arrived, it made you feel a bit as if you were stepping into a museum or temple. The *Delphic Charioteer*, a three-metre-tall white plaster cast (now in the Musée Henri Matisse, Nice-Cimiez) greeted visitors with Olympian majesty. The other rooms in this museum-like space were sparsely furnished with quaint old pieces from various countries. The special light in Matisse's residences in both Nice and Vence – that softened light filtering through the eggshell curtains, half-drawn depending on the position of the sun – created the feeling that one was in a Greek temple where one might lead a monastic life.

A monastic life indeed awaited in the studio of the Boss, at the centre of which the maquette for the future Chapel of the Dominican Nuns in Vence already sat enthroned.

Jacqueline Duhême
Line et les Autres, 1986

In Matisse's studios

From a modest Paris room to his spacious, light-filled atelier in Nice, a look at the artist's workplaces through the years.

The Quai Saint-Michel studio

Matisse's Paris studio at 19, Quai Saint-Michel, where he moved shortly after he arrived in Paris, was 'a medium-sized room with a low ceiling and rather bourgeois furnishings but with a wonderful view', the artist said. The following comment sheds light on his affection for his first studio.

I used to live on Quai Saint-Michel, above Vanier's, Verlaine's publisher. I had two windows. They overlooked the smaller arm of the Seine five stories below. Lovely view: Notre-Dame to the right, the Louvre to the left, the Palais de Justice and Préfecture straight ahead. On Sunday mornings it would always be seething with activity: berthed barges, anglers setting up their little folding chairs, people rummaging through boxes of old books. It was the very heart of Paris.

Henri Matisse
Macula, 1976

The Issy-les-Moulineaux studio

In 1909 Matisse and his family moved into a comfortable house in

The Matisse family moved out of Paris to this comfortable residence in Issy-les-Moulineaux in 1909. The artist had a well-lit studio built in the back.

Issy-les-Moulineaux, on the outskirts of Paris. While not particularly imposing, the house opened out on to a large garden, where the artist immediately had a studio built near an ornamental pool and greenhouse. The Scandinavian critic Ragnar Hoppe interviewed the artist in June 1919 in Paris after his first large postwar exhibition, which had been held at the Bernheim-Jeune gallery the previous month.

'But M. Matisse,' I said, 'you don't have any real compositions here. All I see on the walls are just studies for portraits or sketches made outdoors. Aren't you working on any larger things?'

'Yes, but I can't paint them in this small room here. I need space around me, large dimensions, distance, and that's why I have built myself a studio out in my villa at Issy-les-Moulineaux, where I work on all my decorative projects. There, too, I have a glorious garden with lots of flowers, which for me are by far the best lessons in color composition. The flowers often leave impressions of color indelibly burnt onto my retina. Then, one day when I stand, palette in hand, before a composition and know only approximately which color I should apply, a memory like that may appear in my mind's eye and come to my aid, give me a start. In that way, I, too, become a naturalist, if you can call it naturalist to listen to

The garden and house at Issy-les-Moulineaux.

one's memories and to the selective
instinct that is so closely related to all
creative talent.

'You are welcome to come out
there some day, and you can just call
me up here some afternoon; then we
could keep each other company on
the way. You see, I had a telephone
installed in this little apartment just
today.' We chatted awhile about the
Parisian telephone service, which is
well below the level of the Swedish one,
and parted with a handshake and an
au revoir.

Ragnar Hoppe
'My Visit with Matisse', 1920
trans. in Jack Flam, *Matisse:*
A Retrospective, 1988

The mystery of the *camera lucida*

'A painting must have the power to generate light,' Matisse once told his son-in-law, the scholar Georges Duthuit. The invariably and intensely crystalline quality of colour in Nice was of paramount importance to Matisse, and its 'richness and silvery clarity of

light, especially in the beautiful month of January' influenced his decision to paint there year after year. In the 1940s Louis Aragon – by then a Communist journalist and a poet – became a good friend of Matisse. In his huge, two-volume book on the artist, Aragon records his impressions of his 'demonstration of two truths which have never yet been expressed either in drawing or in painting'.*

This bright room, where in a labyrinthine palace on the heights of Cimiez the great French painter carries out an experiment quite as strange as that of René of Anjou, this *camera lucida* (to use a term from optics) contains at the very least a hundred samples of that experiment, like modulations of a single tune. Henri Matisse, amidst these *completed* images of that which can never be completed, seems himself to be seeking for the explanation of his enterprise while he pursues it.

We find here, indeed, the demonstration of two truths which have never yet been expressed either in drawing or in painting. These are that old saying of Buffon's: *Style is the man himself,* and Gustave Flaubert's wisecrack: *Madame Bovary is myself.…*

The carnival at Nice

The view from Matisse's studio, which stood in the heart of town, transformed the passing show of the outside world into an extension of his work space.

Nice, where he first lived in the Ponchettes district and then on the

Matisse's Hôtel Régina studio – the *camera lucida*, or 'light room' – in 1941. *Themes and Variations* is hanging on the wall.

At the Hôtel Régina, Nice (c. 1950).

heights of Cimiez, is closely associated with the fame of Matisse. This relationship is just as important as any links the painter may have with Mallarmé or Ronsard. It is not a matter of indifference that a great painter should have worked in some particular place; and above all this is true of Matisse.

The reason is this artist's honesty. As I write the word I feel surprise at not having used it before. Honesty is something far more characteristic of Matisse's work than reasonableness. Honesty is often unreasonable.

I can already picture people shrugging their shoulders. The word 'honesty' is usually interpreted as foolishness in a world where illusionism reigns supreme. Too bad; let them drop their shoulders and their illusions. There's no cheating here. The Casino is further down, on the right.

Matisse's windows open on to Nice. In his pictures, I mean. Those marvellous open windows, behind which the sky is as blue as Matisse's eyes behind his spectacles. Here is a dialogue between mirrors. Nice looks at her painter and is imaged in his eyes. A funny sort of Madame Bovary!

If I could only make Matisse say: *'Nice is myself!'* He is too proud for that (I thought *too modest* at first, then I wrote *proud*) and too honest. After all, Flaubert maligned himself: Emma Bovary was not himself. Flaubert was too honest. And not in the least modest.

'Shall I tell you? Nice…why Nice? In my art I have tried to create a setting that will be crystal-clear to the mind; I have found that necessary limpidity in several places in the world, in New York, in Oceania, and at Nice. If I had gone on painting up north, as I did thirty years ago, my painting would have been different; there would have been cloudiness, greys, colours shading off in the distance. Whereas in New York, the painters tell you: One can't paint here, with this metallic sky! And actually it's wonderful! Everything becomes clear, *crystalline*, precise, limpid. Nice helped me in this respect. Understand, the things I paint are objects conceived with plastic means: if I close my eyes I can see the things better than with my eyes open, I see them stripped of their accidental qualities, and that's what I paint…'

Moreover, Nice offered the painter, besides its light and its tropical vegetation, another source of inspiration: no town in France, not even Paris, is more cosmopolitan than Nice, and not only because of the tourists. People have come to Nice from the four corners of the earth, bringing with them the dust of their homeland, their customs and traditions. Thus the town provided Matisse with a choice of models, types of women that he could have found nowhere else, a breath from the wide world outside: the East, Russia, Primitive countries, even the South Seas. The powerful lure is felt throughout his work: a world reconstituted….

Louis Aragon
Henri Matisse: A Novel
trans. Jean Stewart, 1972

'My farm'

A beautiful setting, a regimented day – such was Matisse's idea of a painter's paradise.

Here we are in what I call 'my farm', Matisse informed me. 'I potter here several hours a day, for these plants are a frightful bother to keep up. You have no idea! But as I take care of them, I learn their types, their weight, their flexibility, and that helps me in my drawings….'

'In short, you return to the earth.'

'Yes, of course…why not?' And looking at me over his glasses, he said: 'Do you understand now why I am never bored? For over fifty years I have not stopped working for an instant. From nine o'clock to noon, first sitting. I have lunch. Then I have a little nap and take up my brushes again at two in the afternoon until the evening. You won't believe me. On Sundays, I have to tell all sorts of tales to the models. I promise them that it's the last time I will ever beg them to come and pose on that day. Naturally I pay them double. Finally, when I sense that they are not convinced, I promise them a day off during the week. "But Monsieur Matisse," one of

Matisse in the Vence studio (1946). 'The model…is the source of my energy,' he wrote.

Matisse's aviary, Hôtel Régina, Nice. After the critic and poet André Verdet visited, he wrote, 'There were more than three hundred birds here in this big room. Parakeets, thrushes, pigeons, rare species. They flitted about in aviaries. The pigeons, however, had the run of the room. You'd have thought you were in a forest.'

them answered me, "this has been going on for months and I have never had one afternoon off". Poor things! They don't understand. Nevertheless I can't sacrifice my Sundays for them merely because they have boyfriends. Put yourself in my place: when I was living in the Hôtel de la Mediterranée, the Battle of the Flowers was almost a torture for me. All that music, the floats and the laughter on the Promenade!'

Francis Carco
Conversation with Matisse, 1941
trans. in Jack Flam, *Matisse on Art*, 1973

Matisse the professor

Matisse wrote at length on art. His goal was to be understood. If his writings and statements ultimately comprise a theory, that was not his objective. His comments are our window on his creative process, one which challenged all preconceived notions about method, all formula art. They articulated – in a tone that often struck contemporaries as professorial – 'truth in art' as he saw it.

The role of colour

Suppose I have to paint an interior: I have before me a cupboard; it gives me a sensation of vivid red, and I put down a red which satisfies me. A relation is established between this red and the white of the canvas. Let me put a green near the red, and make the floor yellow; and again there will be relationships between the green or yellow and the white of the canvas which will satisfy me. But these different tones mutually weaken one another. It is necessary that the various marks I use be balanced so that they do not destroy each other. To do this I must organize my ideas; the relationship between the tones must be such that it will sustain and not destroy them. A new combination of colors will succeed the first and render the totality of my representation. I am forced to transpose until finally my picture may seem completely changed when, after successive modifications, the red has succeeded the green as the dominant color. I cannot copy nature in a servile way; I am forced to interpret nature and submit it to the spirit of the picture. From the relationship I have found in all the tones there must result in a living harmony of colors, a harmony analogous to that of a musical composition....

The expressive aspect of colors imposes itself on me in a purely instinctive way. To paint an autumn landscape I will not try to remember what colors suit this season, I will be inspired only by the sensation that the season arouses in me: the icy purity of the sour blue sky will express the season

Matisse at work in 1942.

just as well as the nuances of foliage. My sensation itself may vary, the autumn may be soft and warm like a continuation of summer, or quite cool with a cold sky and lemon-yellow trees that give a chilly impression and already announce winter.

My choice of colors does not rest on any scientific theory; it is based on observation, on sensitivity, on felt experiences. Inspired by certain pages of Delacroix, an artist like Signac is preoccupied with complementary colors, and the theoretical knowledge of them will lead him to use a certain tone in a certain place. But I simply try to put down colors which render my sensation. There is an impelling proportion of tones that may lead me to change the shape of a figure or to transform my composition. Until I have achieved this proportion in all the parts of the composition I strive toward it and keep on working. Then a moment comes when all the parts have found their definite relationships, and from then on it would be impossible for me to add a stroke to my picture without having to repaint it entirely.

In reality, I think that the very theory of complementary colors is not absolute. In studying the paintings of artists whose knowledge of colors depends upon instinct and feeling, and on a constant analogy with their sensations, one could define certain laws of color and so broaden the limits of color theory as it is now defined.

'Notes of a Painter', 1908
trans. in Jack Flam, *Matisse: A Retrospective*, 1988

To achieve a direct and pure translation of emotion, one must be thoroughly familiar with the entire range of means

and try them out to see how effective they really are. Young artists shouldn't be afraid of making mistakes. Painting involves ceaseless exploration as well as an adventure of the most bewildering kind? When I was a student, there were times when I tried to obtain a certain balance and expressive rhythm with nothing but colours; there were other times when I investigated the power of arabesque alone. And whenever colour became overly intense, I would tone it

Reclining Nude Seen From the Back (1938).

down – which is not to say I made it darker – so that my forms would acquire greater stability and definition. So what if you drift, if each time you do so you make some headway?

from Gaston Diehl
Peintres d'Aujourd'hui, 1943

To say that colour has once again become expressive is to write its history. For a long time colour was only the complement of drawing. Raphael, Mantegna, or Dürer, like all Renaissance painters, constructed with drawing first and then added colour.

On the other hand, the Italian primitives and especially the Orientals, had made colour a means of expression. …It was with some reason that Ingres was called an 'unknown Chinese in Paris', since he was the first to use bold colours, limiting them without distorting them.

From Delacroix to Van Gogh and especially Gauguin, through the Impressionists, who cleared the way, and Cézanne, who gave the definitive impulse and introduced coloured volumes, one can follow this rehabilitation of the role of colour, and the restitution of its emotive power.

'The Role and Modalities of Colour,' from Gaston Diehl *Problèmes de la Peinture*, 1945 trans. in Jack Flam, *Matisse on Art*, 1973

Sculpture

I took up sculpture because what interested me in painting was a clarification of my ideas. I changed my method, and worked in clay in order to have a rest from painting where I had done absolutely all that I could do for the time being. That is to say that it was done for the purpose of organization, to put order into my feelings, and find a style to suit me. When I found it in sculpture, it helped me in my painting. It was always in view of a complete possession of my mind, a sort of hierarchy of all my sensations, that I kept working in the hope of finding an ultimate method.

from Jean Guichard-Meili *Matisse* trans. Caroline Moorehead, 1967

Composition and expression

What I am after, above all, is expression. Sometimes it has been conceded that I have a certain technical ability but all the same my ambition is limited, and does not go beyond the purely visual satisfaction such as can be obtained from looking at a picture. But the thought of a painter must not be considered as separate from his pictorial means, for the thought is worth no more than its expression by the means, which must be more complete (and by complete I do not mean complicated) the deeper is his thought. I am unable to distinguish between the feeling I have about life and my way of translating it….

Expression, for me, does not reside in passions glowing in a human face or manifested by violent movement. The entire arrangement of my picture is expressive: the place occupied by the figures, the empty spaces around them, the proportions, everything has its share. Composition is the art of arranging in a decorative manner the diverse elements at the painter's command to express his feelings. In a picture every part will be visible and will play its appointed role, whether it be principal or secondary. Everything that is not useful in the picture is, it follows, harmful. A work of art must be harmonious in its entirety: any superfluous detail would replace some other essential detail in the mind of the spectator.

Composition, the aim of which should be expression, is modified according to the surface to be covered. If I take a sheet of paper of a given size, my drawing will have a necessary relationship to its format. I would not repeat this drawing on another sheet of different proportions, for example, rectangular instead of square.

'Notes of a Painter', 1908 trans. in Jack Flam, *Matisse: A Retrospective*, 1988

The substance of things

However, with a still life consisting of a seashell, a blue flowerpot, a coffee cup, a coffee pot and three green apples on a black and green marble table – which I laboured over (transformed) during thirty sessions – I believe I've done all I can possibly do in the abstract direction – by dint of meditation, trying out higher or lower points of view, paring (I hope you understand me, or rather that I am making myself understood). For now I can't go any further, I can't even repeat myself, that's out of the question. So I've been disciplining myself to adopt a less extraordinary, less disembodied approach – and I have moved closer to the substance of things. To that end I've painted some oysters. There, my dear fellow, taste sensations are a must. In a picture an oyster has to be itself a little; a bit of Dutch rendering is called for. This is the third canvas I've done of this subject. Of course, try though I may to fight the urge, I take into account the room, the surrounding space. I've given myself free rein. It has required a great effort on my part, and I have come to rediscover natural qualities, ones that I had to curb for a long time, the tang of delectable painting, which I think you'll find interesting. I don't know what it will lead to, I'm not sure of the value of what I've just done, the child has just been born. But I am sure that these paintings, while vividly coloured, can be rendered only with oils, whereas for a long time I only cared about lines and colours, the medium – watercolour, gouache, what have you – was immaterial to me. All that mattered was the expressive blending of variously coloured and proportioned surfaces. I think that's progress. I wish I could live long enough to return to my earlier approach and see what my recent work might add to it.

Henri Matisse to Théodore Palady
7 December 1940

Still Life with Shell by Hélène Adant, Hôtel Régina (1940).

That magic ingredient

Suppose I want to paint a woman's body: first of all I imbue it with grace and charm, but I know that I must give something more. I will condense the meaning of this body by seeking its essential lines. The charm will be less apparent at first glance, but it must eventually emerge from the new image which will have a broader meaning, one more fully human.

'Notes of a Painter', 1908
trans. in Jack Flam, *Matisse: A Retrospective*, 1988

Following the clues

What torture life is when someone as acutely sensitive as I am depends on a method, or rather when acute sensitivity prevents one from relying on a method for support. It's completely undone me, but I'm reminded that it's been like that my entire life – a moment of despair followed by a happy flash of revelation that allows me to accomplish something that transcends reason…. I am bent on following the clues that are bound logically to lead me to express myself in ways I feel I am exceptional, using means (colours) richer than line drawing, with which I bring out the part of nature that moves me, in the sympathy I create between the objects around me, around which I live, and in which ultimately I invest my feelings of affection – without risking the pain, as one does in life.

Henri Matisse to André Rouveyre
6 October 1941

Straight from the heart

I'm an old crackpot who wishes to make a fresh start in painting so that I may finally die content. And yet, that's impossible. Since I want my painting to more closely correspond to my drawings – the ones that come straight from the heart, done with the utmost simplicity – I have started down a gruelling road that seems inordinately long because of the little time remaining to me at my age. And yet, for the sake of self-consistency, I cannot do otherwise. Given the kind of colour relations I tend to use to render what I feel, independent of surface reality, I find myself representing objects without perspective, I mean, viewed frontally – in very close proximity – connected to one another by my feelings – in an atmosphere created by the magical relations of colour. Why not, to be logical, use nothing but local colours – without reflections – and human figures all on the same plane as in [the children's game of Aunt Sally]? And, on these simplified elements of representation, apply a colour derived from sublimated local colour, or even completely dreamed up, according to the emotion the very presence of nature arouses in me? But in my synthetic drawing I am leaving room for surface reality. I even benefit from it. Certain secondary elements are as useful to me as essential ones.

Henri Matisse to André Rouveyre
3 June 1947

Line and emotion

My line drawing is the purest and most direct translation of my emotion. The simplification of the medium allows that. At the same time, these drawings are more complete than they may appear to some people who confuse them with a sketch. They generate light; seen on a dull day or in indirect light they contain, in addition to the quality and sensitivity of line, light and value differences which quite clearly correspond to color. These qualities are also evident to many in full light. They derive from the fact that the drawings are always preceded by studies made in a less rigorous medium than pure line, such as charcoal or stump drawing, which enables me to consider simultaneously the character of the model, the human expression, the quality of surrounding light, atmosphere and all that can only be expressed by drawing. And only when I feel drained by the effort, which may go on for several sessions, can I with a clear mind and without hesitation, give free rein to my pen. Then I feel clearly that my emotion is expressed in plastic writing. Once my emotive line has modeled the light of my white paper without destroying its precious whiteness, I can neither add nor take anything away. The page is written; no correction is possible. If it is not adequate, there is no alternative to but to begin again, as if it were an acrobatic feat....

I have never considered drawing as an exercise of particular dexterity, rather as principally a means of expressing intimate feelings and describing states of mind, but a means deliberately simplified so as to give simplicity and spontaneity to the expression which should speak without clumsiness, directly to the mind of the spectator.

My models, human figures, are never just 'extras' in an interior. They are the principal theme in my work. I depend entirely on my model, whom I observe at liberty, and then I decide on the pose which best suits *her nature*. When I take a new model, I intuit the pose that will best suit her from her

P*ortrait of Mme Matisse* (1915).

unselfconscious attitudes of repose, and then I become the slave of that pose. I often keep those girls several years, until my interest is exhausted. My plastic signs probably express their souls (a word I dislike), which interests me subconsciously, or what else is there? Their forms are not always perfect, but they are always expressive. The emotional interest aroused in me by them does not appear particularly in the representation of their bodies, but often rather in the lines or the special values distributed over the whole canvas or paper, which forms its complete orchestration, its architecture. But not everyone perceives this. It is perhaps sublimated sensual pleasure, which may not yet be perceived by everyone.

Someone called me 'this charmer who takes pleasure in charming monsters'. I never thought of my creations as charmed or charming monsters.

I replied to someone who said I didn't see women as I represented them: 'If I met such women in the street, I should run away in terror.' Above all, I do not create a woman, *I make a picture*.

In spite of the absence of shadows or half-tones expressed by hatching, I do not renounce the play of values or modulations. I modulate with variations in the weight of line, and above all with the areas it delimits on the white paper. I modify the different parts of the white paper without touching them, but by their relationships. This can be clearly seen in the drawings of Rembrandt, Turner and of colorists in general.

To sum up, I work *without a theory*. I am conscious only of the forces I use, and I am driven on by an idea which I really only grasp as it grows with the picture. As Chardin used to say, 'I add (or I take away, because I scrape out a lot) until it looks right.'

Making a picture would seem as logical as building a house, if one worked on sound principles. One should not bother about the *human* side. Either one has it or one hasn't. If one has, it colors the work in spite of everything.

'Notes of a Painter on His Drawing,'
Le Point, July 1939
trans. in Jack Flam, *Matisse:
A Retrospective*, 1988

'I am led'

When I make my drawings – 'Variations' – the path traced by my pencil on the sheet of paper is, to some extent, analogous to the gesture of a man groping his way in the darkness. I mean that there is nothing foreseen about my path: I am led. I do not lead. I go from one point in the thing which is my model to another point which I always see in isolation, independent of the other points towards which my pen will subsequently move. I am simply guided by an interior impulse which I translate as it takes shape, rather than by the exterior on which my eyes are fixed yet which has no more importance for me than a feeble glimmer in the darkness, towards which I have to make my way first – and then, having reached it, I perceive another gleam towards which I shall move, constantly inventing my way thither. The way is so interesting, isn't it the most interesting part of the performance?

Just as the spider throws out (or fastens?) its thread to some convenient protuberance and thence to another that it perceives, and from one point to another weaves its web.

As for the way I draw my studies, my 'Themes', my action has not yet appeared so clearly to me, because it is far more complex and very deliberate. This 'deliberateness' is a serious obstacle to the perception of what is most important – because it prevents instinct from emerging unmistakably.

Louis Aragon
Henri Matisse: A Novel
trans. Jean Stewart, 1972

'We belong to our time'

Rules have no existence outside of individuals: otherwise a good professor would be as great a genius as Racine. Any one of us is capable of repeating fine maxims, but few can also penetrate their meaning. I am ready to admit that from a study of the works of Raphael or Titian a more complete set of rules can be drawn than from the works of Manet or Renoir, but the rules followed by Manet and Renoir were those which suited their temperaments and I prefer the most minor of their paintings to all the work of those who are content to imitate the *Venus of Urbino* or the *Madonna of the Goldfinch*. These latter are of no value to anyone, for whether we want to or not, we belong to our time and we share in its opinions, its feelings, even its delusions. All artists bear the imprint of their time, but the great artists are those in whom this is most profoundly marked. Our epoch for instance is better represented by Courbet than by Flandrin, by Rodin better than Frémiet. Whether we like it or not, however insistently we call ourselves exiles, between our period and ourselves an indissoluble bond is established, and M. [Mérodack] Peladan [a writer who criticized his work] himself cannot escape it. The aestheticians of the future may perhaps use his books as evidence if they get it in their heads to prove that no one of our time understood anything about the art of Leonardo da Vinci.

'Notes of a Painter', 1908
trans. in Jack Flam, *Matisse:
A Retrospective*, 1988

How a painting is born

Often when I start to work I record fresh and superficial sensations during the first session. A few years ago I was sometimes satisfied with the result. But today if I were satisfied with this, now that I think I can see further, my picture would have a vagueness in it: I should have recorded the fugitive sensations of a moment which could not completely define my feelings and which I should barely recognize the next day.

I want to reach that state of condensation of sensations which makes a painting. I might be satisfied with a

work done at one sitting, but I would soon tire of it; therefore, I prefer to rework it so that later I may recognize it as representative of my state of mind. There was a time when I never left my paintings hanging on the wall because they reminded me of moments of overexcitement and I did not like to see them again when I was calm. Nowadays I try to put serenity into my pictures and rework them as long as I have not succeeded.

'Notes of a Painter,' 1908
trans. in Jack Flam, *Matisse:
A Retrospective*, 1988

Look long and well

When painting, first look long and well at your model or subject, and decide on your general color scheme. This must prevail. In painting a landscape you choose it for certain beauties – spots of color, suggestions of composition. Close your eyes and visualize the picture; then go to work, always keeping these characteristics the important features of the picture. And you must at once indicate all that you would have in the complete work. All must be considered in interrelation during the process – nothing can be added.

One must stop from time to time to consider the subject (model, landscape, etc.) in its ensemble. What you are aiming for, above all, is unity.

Order above all, in color. Put three or four touches of color that you have understood, upon the canvas; add another, if you can – if you can't, set this canvas aside and begin again.

From the notebook of Sarah Stein,
one of Matisse's students, c. 1908
trans. in Jack Flam, *Matisse:
A Retrospective*, 1988

In Matisse's wake

Matisse enjoyed learning, and, for a while, teaching. How did he treat younger artists? And what did he make of their work?

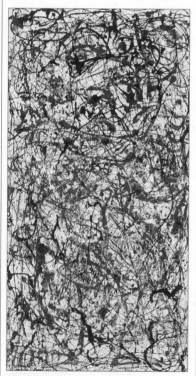

Jackson Pollock, *Number 26A 'Black and White'* (1948).

From Renoir to Pollock

Matisse took more notice of younger generations than Picasso did, and he was less judgmental about emerging trends.

One day when we were visiting Matisse, he showed us some catalogs he had received from his son Pierre, an art dealer in New York. They contained reproductions of paintings by Jackson Pollock and others of that persuasion.

'I have the impression that I'm incapable of judging painting like that,' Matisse said after we had finished looking at the catalogs, 'for the simple reason that one is always unable to judge fairly what follows one's own work. One can judge what has happened before and what comes along at the same time. And even among those who follow, when a painter hasn't completely forgotten me I understand him a little bit, even though he goes beyond me. But when he gets to the point where he no longer makes any reference to what for me is painting, I can no longer understand him. I can't judge him, either. It's completely over my head.

'When I was young, I was very fond of Renoir's painting. Toward the end of the First World War, I found myself in the Midi. Renoir was still living, but very old. I still admired him and I decided to call on him at *Les Collettes*, his place at Cagnes. He received me in very friendly fashion and so, after a few more visits, I brought him a few of my paintings, to find out what he thought of them. He looked them over with a somewhat disapproving air. Finally he said, "Well, I must speak the truth. I must say I don't like what you do, for various reasons. I should almost like to say that you're not really a good painter, or even that you're a very bad painter. But there's one thing that prevents me from telling you that. When you put on some black, it stays right there on the canvas. All my life I have been saying that one can't any longer use black without making a hole in the canvas. It's not a color. Now, you speak the language of color. Yet you put on black and you make it stick. So even though I don't like at all what you do, and my inclination would be to tell you you're a bad painter, I suppose you are a painter, after all." '

Matisse smiled. 'You see, it's very difficult to understand and appreciate the generation that follows. Little by little, as one goes through life, one creates not only a language for himself, but an aesthetic doctrine along with it. That is, at the same time one establishes for himself the values that he creates, he establishes them, at least to a degree, in an absolute sense. And so it becomes all the more difficult for one to understand a kind of painting whose point of departure lies beyond one's own point of arrival. It's something that's based on completely different foundations. When we arrive on the scene, the movement of painting for a moment contains us, swallows us up, and we add, perhaps, a little link to the chain. Then the movement continues on past us and we are outside it and we don't understand it any longer.'

Pablo said, with a sarcastic air, 'Ah, well, then we pretend to be Buddhists – some of us, at least.' He shook his head. 'I don't agree with you at all,' he said. 'And I don't *care* whether I'm in a good position to judge what comes after me. I'm against that sort of stuff. As far as these new painters are concerned, I think it is a mistake to let oneself go

completely and lose oneself in the gesture. Giving oneself up entirely to the action of painting – there's something in that which displeases me enormously. It's not at all that I hold to a rational conception of painting – I have nothing in common, for example, with a man like Poussin – but in any case the unconscious is so strong in us that it expresses itself in one fashion or another. Those are the roots through which the whole human substratum communicates itself from one being to another. Whatever we may do, it expresses itself in spite of us. So why should we deliberately hand ourselves over to it?'

Françoise Gilot and Carlton Lake
Life with Picasso, 1965

On abstraction

Matisse answered the question 'Do you think that today's abstract art could lead to a dead end?'

First of all, I will say that there is no one abstract art. All art is abstract in itself when it is the fundamental expression stripped of all anecdote. But let's not play on words…Non-figurative art, then…

All the same, one can say that today if there is no longer any need for painting to give explanations in its physical make-up, yet the artist who is expressing the object by a synthesis, while seeming to depart from it, must nonetheless be able to explain this object himself *to himself*. He must necessarily end by forgetting it, but I repeat, deep *within himself* he must have a real memory of the object and of the reactions it produces in his mind. One starts off with an object. Sensation follows. One doesn't start from a void. Nothing is gratuitous. As for the so-called abstract painters of today, it seems to me that too many of them depart from a void. They are gratuitous, they have no power, no inspiration, no feeling, they defend a non-existent point of view: they imitate abstraction.

One doesn't find any expression in what is supposed to be the relationship of their colours. If they can't create relationships they can use all the colours in vain.

Rapport is the affinity between things, the common language; rapport is love, yes love.

Without rapport, without this love, there is no longer any criterion of observation and thus there is no longer any work of art.

from André Verdet
Interview with Henri Matisse, 1952
trans. in Jack Flam, *Matisse on Art*, 1973

Masson on Matisse

The French Surrealist artist describes the painter.

The man was larger than life! Larger than life, he came across as a bit unemotional, stiff…. A very unemotional, serious-minded, detached man, right? Serious-minded. Just the same, I thought it very pleasing back then that he could take notice of a painter far younger than he, take more than just a cursory interest in his work. In other words, he'd keep his eye on me, warily, inquire about my approach, whereupon I would make the same inquiries of him….

André Masson
Conversation with Georges Charbonnier
1958

Matisse in the villa Le Rêve, Vence.

A teacher on teaching

Matisse explains why he opened, and later closed, his school.

I thought it would be good for young artists to avoid the road I traveled myself. I thus took the initiative of opening a school…. Many students appeared. I forced myself to correct each one, taking into account the spirit in which his efforts were conceived. I especially took pains to inculcate in them a sense of tradition. Needless to say, many of my students were disappointed to see that a master with a reputation for being revolutionary could have repeated the words of Courbet to them: 'I have

'What do I want?'

The choices and responsibilities of youth.

The young painter who cannot free himself from the influence of the preceding generation is bound to be swallowed up.

In order to protect himself from the spell of the work of his immediate predecessors whom he admires, he can search for new sources of inspiration in the production of diverse civilizations, according to his own affinities....

If he is sensitive, no painter can lose the contribution of the preceding generation because it is part of him, despite himself. Yet it is necessary for him to disengage himself in order to produce in his own turn something new and freshly inspired....

A young painter should realize that he does not have to invent everything, but that he should above all get things straight in his mind by reconciling the different points of view expressed in the beautiful works of art by which he is affected, and at the same time by directly questioning nature.

After he has become acquainted with his means of expression, the painter should ask himself, 'What do I want?' and proceed in his researches, both simple and complex, to try to find it.

If he can preserve his sincerity toward his deeper sentiment without trickery or without being too lenient with himself, his curiosity will not desert him, and he will therefore have in his old age the same ardour for hard work and the necessity to learn that he had when young. What could be better!

'Observations on Painting'
Verve, December 1945
trans. in Jack Flam, *Matisse on Art*, 1973

simply wished to assert the reasoned and independent feeling of my own individuality within a total knowledge of tradition.'

The effort I made to penetrate the thinking of each one tired me out. I reached the point where I thought a student was heading in the wrong direction and he told me (revenge of my masters), 'That's the way I think.' The saddest part was that they could not conceive that I was depressed to see them 'doing Matisse'. Then I understood that I had to choose between being a painter and a teacher. I soon closed my school.

from Jacques Guenne, 'A Conversation with Henri Matisse',
L'Art Vivant, 15 September 1925
trans. in Jack Flam, *Matisse: A Retrospective*, 1988

FURTHER READING

Aragon, Louis, *Henri Matisse: A Novel*, 2 vols., trans. Jean Stewart, 1972

Barr, Jr., Alfred H., *Matisse: His Art and his Public*, 1951

Bonnard/Matisse: Letters Between Friends, 1925–1946, trans. Richard Howard, 1992

Carlson, Victor I., *Matisse as a Draughtsman*, 1971

Cowart, Jack, and Dominique Fourcade, *Henri Matisse: The Early Years in Nice, 1916–1930*, 1986

Cowart, Jack, et al., *Matisse in Morocco: The Paintings and Drawings, 1912–1913*, 1992

Delectorskaya, Lydia, *With Apparent Ease...: Henri Matisse – Paintings from 1935–1939*, 1988

Duthuit, Claude, ed., *Catalogue Raisonné des Ouvrages Illustrés*, 1987

Duthuit-Matisse, Marguerite, and Claude Duthuit, *Henri Matisse: Catalogue Raisonné de l'Oeuvre Gravé*, 2 vols., 1983

Elderfield, John, *The Drawings of Henri Matisse*, 1984

——, *Henri Matisse: A Retrospective*, 1992

——, *Matisse in the Collection of The Museum of Modern Art*, 1978

Elsen, Albert E., *The Sculpture of Henri Matisse*, 1972

Escholier, Raymond, *Matisse: A Portrait of the Artist and the Man*, 1960

Flam, Jack D., *Matisse: The Man and his Art, 1869–1918*, 1987

Flam, Jack D., ed., *Matisse: A Retrospective*, 1988

——, *Matisse on Art*, 1973

Gilot, Françoise, *Matisse and Picasso: A Friendship in Art*, 1990

Gilot, Françoise, and Carlton Lake, *Life with Picasso*, 1965

Gowing, Lawrence, *Matisse*, 1979

Guichard-Meili, Jean, *Matisse: Paper Cut-Outs*, 1984

Hahnloser, Margrit, *Matisse: The Graphic Work*, 1988

Monod-Fontaine, Isabelle, *Matisse*, 1989

——, *The Sculpture of Henri Matisse*, 1984

Richardson, Brenda, *Dr Claribel and Miss Etta: The Cone Collection of the Baltimore Museum of Art*, 1985

Schneider, Pierre, *Matisse*, trans. Michael Taylor and Bridget Stevens Romer, 1984

Wattenmaker, Richard, et al., *Great French Paintings from the Barnes Collection*, 1993

LIST OF ILLUSTRATIONS

INDEX

A scene from Matisse's Venice studio.

ACKNOWLEDGMENTS

The publishers wish to thank Claude Duthuit, Wanda de Guebriant, Jacqueline Duhême and Any-Claude Medioni.

PHOTO CREDITS

TEXT CREDITS

Xavier Girard
is the curator of the Musée Matisse,
Nice-Cimiez. He has taught art history
at the University of Nice, written criticism for
Art Press, Art Forum and *Galeries Magazine,* and
served on exhibition committees
at museums in and outside France.
He has written books on European painting and
sculpture and in 1986 created the continuing series
Cahiers Henri Matisse.
He has organized Matisse exhibitions
in France, Italy, Switzerland and Japan.

© Gallimard 1993

English translation copyright © Editions Gallimard 1994

Works by Henri Matisse © Succession H. Matisse

Translated by I. Mark Paris

First distributed in 1994 by Thames and Hudson Ltd, London

British Library Cataloguing-in-Publication Data

A catalogue record for this book is available from
the British Library

ISBN 0–500–30046–1

Printed and bound in Italy
by Editoriale Libraria, Trieste